SKELETON KEYS

THE LEGEND OF GAP-TOOTH JACK

D1078081

To the real Emily ~ Guy Bass

To Mackenzie G – sorry about the wait
~ Pete Williamson

STRIPES PUBLISHING LIMITED

An imprint of the Little Tiger Group
1 Coda Studios, 189 Munster Road,
London SW6 6AW

A paperback original
First published in Great Britain in 2020

Text copyright © Guy Bass, 2020
Illustrations copyright © Pete Williamson, 2020

ISBN: 978-1-78895-246-0

The right of Guy Bass and Pete Williamson to be identified as the
author and illustrator of this work respectively has been asserted by
them in accordance with the Copyright, Designs and Patents Act, 1988.

All rights reserved.

This book is sold subject to the condition that it shall not, by
way of trade or otherwise, be lent, resold, hired out, or otherwise
circulated without the publisher's prior consent in any form of
binding or cover other than that in which it is published and
without a similar condition including this condition being
imposed upon the subsequent purchaser.

A CIP catalogue record for this book is available
from the British Library.

Printed and bound in the UK.

The Forest Stewardship Council® (FSC®) is a global, not-for-profit organization
dedicated to the promotion of responsible forest management worldwide.
FSC® defines standards based on agreed principles for responsible forest stewardship
that are supported by environmental, social, and economic stakeholders.
To learn more, visit www.fsc.org

2 4 6 8 10 9 7 5 3 1

SKELETON KEYS

THE LEGEND OF GAP-TOOTH JACK

WRITTEN BY
GUY BASS

ILLUSTRATED BY
PETE WILLIAMSON

LITTLE TIGER
LONDON

The Key to
Reality

The Key to
Second Sight

The Key to
Doorminion

The Forbidden Key

The Key to Time

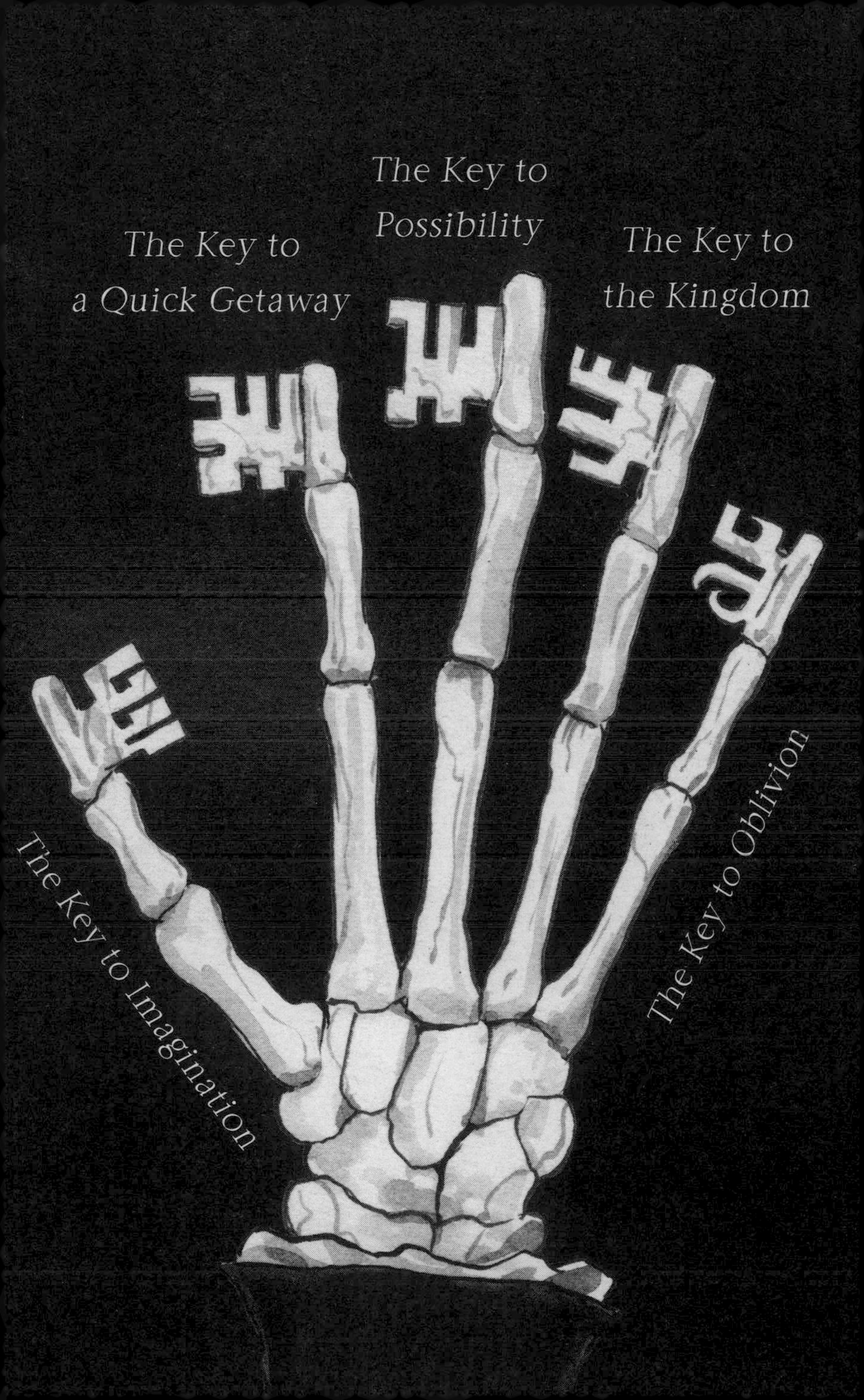
The Key to
a Quick Getaway
The Key to
Possibility
The Key to
the Kingdom
The Key to Imagination
The Key to Oblivion

Greetings! To tick-tockers, swiss-cheesers and hurlypots! To the imaginary and the unimaginary! To the living, the dead and everyone in between, my name is Keys ... Skeleton Keys.

Ages or so ago, long before you were even thinking about being born, I was an IF – an imaginary friend. Then, before I knew what was happening, I was suddenly as real as a dog's tail! I had become *unimaginary*.

But that was a lifetime or three ago. Nowadailies, I concern myself with those IFs who have been recently *unimagined*. Wherever they may appear, so does Ol' Mr Keys! For these fantabulant fingers of mine open doors to anywhere and elsewhere ... hidden worlds ... secret places ... doors to the limitless realm of all imagination.

O, glorious burden! These keys have opened more doors than you have had biscuits – and each door has led to an adventure that would make a head spin from its neck! The stories I could tell you...

But of course you would not be here if you did not want a story! Well, never fear, dallywanglers – today I have a hum-dum-dinger of a tale to make even the soundest mind loop-de-loop! Brace your breeches for the truly unbelievable, unbelievably true tale I have called *The Legend of Gap-tooth Jack*.

Ah, Gap-tooth Jack – thief! Adventurer! Champion of imagining! Jack was a friend to some, hero to others, and a right pain in the rumplings for everyfolk else. The flabbergasting fable of Gap-tooth Jack is even older than I, but to find our way to the past we must begin in the present, with a *second* story, and a boy named Kasper.

Kasper has what we in the business of imagining call a *wild imagination*. On the

seventh day of his seventh year,
Kasper imagined himself a
friend. He did not *need*
to, perhaps, for he had
friends enough. But
imaginations are not
trussed 'n' tethered by
need ... imaginations run
free! Kasper named his IF
Wordy Gerdy. Gerdy was
a ghost of a girl with a most
remarkable ability – with pen in
hand she could rewrite the story of
life itself. Let us suppose you have a
pet dog – if Wordy Gerdy rewrote your
story, you might suddenly have a *cat*
instead. And, what is more, you would not
even know that anything had changed –
you would be as sure as shampoo that
you had *always* had a cat!

Now imagine if Wordy Gerdy became unimaginary – if her power to rewrite stories became real. What then is to stop chaos, confusion or even calamity? For strange things can happen when imaginations run wild...

Join me as I begin to unravel the mystery of the myth of the legend of Gap-tooth Jack, by first paying a much needed visit to Kasper and his family. Their house, dwarfed by the sprawling city that surrounds it, shuddles 'n' shakes as a thunderstorm rages outside. The story has just begun, and yet it has already been rewritten...

CHAPTER ONE

REWRITTEN

(MEET THE FAMILY)

"With the turn of a key, the adventure begins."
—*SK*

K NOCK.
 KNOCK.
  KNOCK.

Kasper was lying on the living-room floor, watching his third-favourite episode of *Howie Howzer's Haunted Trousers*, when the knock came.

"*Mu-um*," he called, not taking his eyes off the television. The sound of the thunderstorm outside swallowed his call. "*Da-ad*, someone's at the *dooooooor...*"

There was no answer from the kitchen. Kasper wasn't about to move – not with the episode reaching its haunting highpoint. He turned up the volume as thunder clapped outside.

Then:

CLICK CLUNK.

A key turned in the lock.

Kasper sat up. Everyone was in the kitchen – Mum, Dad, Jakob, the twins.

So, who was unlocking the front door?

A cold shiver ran down Kasper's back. He got to his feet and turned to see the door creak slowly open. Rain lashed in as lightning forked in the night sky, illuminating a tall, lean figure standing in the doorway.

"Forgive my intrudings," the figure said. "I fear that if I do not come in, I might drown in this thundersome weather."

The figure took off a wide, three-peaked hat to reveal a grinning, bone-white skull.

Kasper gasped and stumbled backwards until he was pressed against the television.

"Fret not, I am not so spine-chillering as I look," the skeleton said as he stepped inside. "I am afraid skinless is how I came into this world, so skinless is how I remain."

Kasper tried to call out but fear caught the cry in his throat.

"My name is Keys ... Skeleton Keys," the skeleton continued, placing his hat on the nearby sofa and shaking the raindrops from his coat. "And you need to be afeared. After all, *you* brought me here."

"I-I did?" Kasper blurted.

"Well, *someone* did," replied Skeleton Keys, glancing around. "For although I was far that-a-way in the comfort of my Doorminion, I felt the *twitch*, that most soul-clattering rattle of the bones that alerts me to a new *unimagining*."

"I-I don't understand," Kasper replied.

"Somewhere in this house is an IF – an imaginary friend – that has been brought to life!" the skeleton declared. "Have you not noticed anything oddish or outlandish of late? Unimaginary friends do tend to be accompanied by the most flabbergasting freakery..."

"I don't know what you— Wait." Kasper scratched the back of his head, the fog of fear clearing a little. "Like what happened to Wordy Gerdy?" he asked.

"Who?"

"M-my friend – I mean, not my real friend," Kasper replied. "Except now she is."

"Now she is your real friend, or now she is *real*?" Skeleton Keys asked, leaning towards him.

"*Really* real," Kasper explained.

"How real? As real as a vivid dream? As real as a stubbed toe? As real as rock cakes?"

"I was thinking about her and all of a sudden she wasn't in my head any more – she was right there in front of me. She was—"

"Unimaginary," Skeleton Keys interrupted. "I knew it, my twitch was right on the money! Now tell me, Kasper, where is this Wordy Gerdy?"

Kasper pointed to a door at the far end of the room. "In the kitchen, with everyone else."

"Then fret not – Ol' Mr Keys is on the case," declared Skeleton Keys, taking long, deliberate strides towards the kitchen. He pushed open the door and strode inside to find Kasper's family sitting around a small, white table. "Dogs 'n' cats!" the skeleton gasped.

"Mum, Dad, this, uh, this is Mr Keys," said Kasper, following in behind.

"How do you do, Mr Keys?" said Kasper's mum. "May I offer you a cup of tea?"

"I am afraid it would have nowhere to go,"

replied Skeleton Keys. "Thank you all the same."

"Then something to eat?" added Kasper's mum.

"CARROTS!" cried Kasper's dad.

"It's always carrots with you," sighed Kasper's mum.

Skeleton Keys scratched his skull with a key-tipped finger, before ushering Kasper to a corner of the kitchen.

"Forgive me for asking," he whispered. "But are you *sure* this is your family?"

"What? Yeah," replied Kasper. "What do you mean?"

"It is just that I could not help but notice that your father is a *very large rabbit*."

Kasper looked at his dad. Sure enough, he was a brown-grey rabbit the size of a bear

Kasper shrugged. "What else would he be?" he said.

"CARROTS! CARROTS!"

shouted the enormous rabbit, thumping his great foot against the floor.

"I also note," Skeleton Keys continued, "that your mother is, well, is—"

"Is what?" Kasper's mother interrupted. She stood on the kitchen table, her hands on her hips. She was no taller than a teacup. "These are modern times, Mr Keys. Families come in all shapes and sizes."

"Quite so, but…" uttered the skeleton, gazing in bafflement at a pair of hamster-sized, sky-blue elephants, huddled together in a high chair on the other side of the table.

"That's Sofie and Ingrid – they're twins," Kasper explained as both elephants let out an identical trumpeting sound. Then he pointed to a sock puppet with buttons for eyes, draped lifelessly on the kitchen table. "And that's my big brother, Jakob."

"Don't mind him, you'll be lucky to get two words out of him all year," Kasper's tiny mother tutted as Skeleton Keys leaned in to inspect the sock puppet. "You know what teenagers are like."

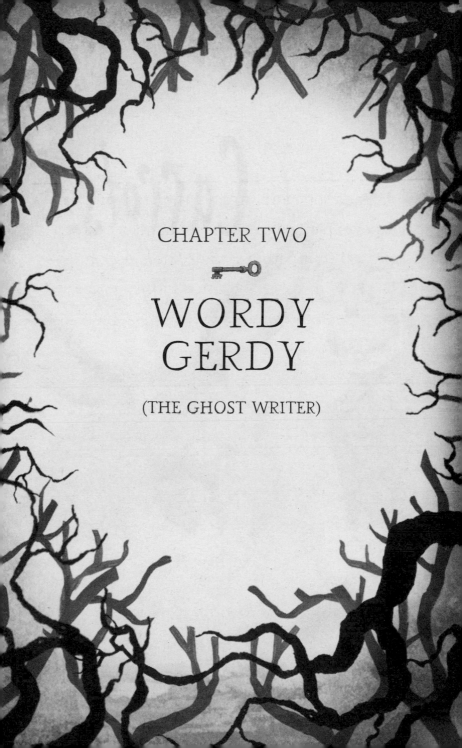

CHAPTER TWO

WORDY GERDY

(THE GHOST WRITER)

*"Imagination never fails!
But no one else should write your tales"*
—SK

"*C*rumcrinkles..." said Skeleton Keys, gazing around the room at Kasper's decidedly unconventional family. "Who did all this?"

"Did all what?" Kasper asked.

"CARROTS!" boomed Kasper's dad.

"Why, this! And this and this, and, by my buckles, *this*," Skeleton Keys cried, pointing at each of Kasper's family members in turn. "Who transformed, transmogrified and transfigured these poor dallywanglers? You are not trying to tell me that your father has *always* been a rabbit?"

"Always...?" replied Kasper as if the word had suddenly illuminated a hidden memory. "I mean, I-I don't remember him being anything else. But I guess I don't really *remember* him being a rabbit either."

"I do believe you are as confuddled as your family is converted ... and that this is the work of an *unimaginary*," declared Skeleton Keys, craning low to eyeball Kasper. "Where is your IF, Kasper? Where is—"

"Didn't do it!"

The cry came from inside a low cupboard at the far end of the kitchen. Skeleton Keys tilted his head with a dry creak, his milk-white eyeballs fixing upon a rattling cupboard door. He reached the cupboard in two long strides. It rattled again as he wrapped his key-tipped fingers around the door handle.

"Wordy Gerdy? Is that—"

"DIDN'T DO IT!"

The cupboard doors were suddenly flung open from the inside, sending Skeleton Keys flying. A strange, ghostly girl burst from within and hovered, impossibly, in the air. She flitted around the room in panic before finally settling in the far corner of the kitchen, like a bee exhausted from buzzing around a window. Though she was solid enough, the girl was faintly see-through and emitted a greenish-white glow.

"Wordy Gerdy, I presume," said Skeleton Keys, dusting himself off.

"Gerdy didn't do it! Gerdy didn't change a thing! Everything like this already!" The ghoulish girl hovered in the air again, her hair floating above her head as if she was underwater. In her right hand, she held a large, brush-tipped pen.

"Cheese 'n' biscuits! She is a *ghost writer?*" Skeleton Keys gasped, a peel of thunder echoing outside. "Well, that explains *everything.*"

"*What* explains everything?" asked Kasper as his unimaginary friend hid her pen behind her back.

"Yours is a wild and wonderfilled mind, Kasper," he said. "After all, what more fantabulant friend could you wish for, than one who could change everything ... a friend who could *rewrite* the story of your life? Why, you could be anything you want! An explorer ... a swashbuckler ... a run-for-fun, swing-a-sword gadabout who lives only for adventure!"

"But—" Kasper began.

"CARROTS!" bellowed Kasper's dad.

"But then you imagined your IF so wildly and so well that she suddenly became as real as wrapping paper," continued Skeleton Keys. "You made Wordy Gerdy *unimaginary*, Kasper. And now her ability to rewrite stories is as real as she!"

"Don't listen!" Wordy Gerdy wailed.

"I-I don't understand..." Kasper said, hot with panic.

"The pen is the tool for creation – words flow from the mind to the pen like water from a tap ... but your IF's pen has a peculiar power," Skeleton Keys explained. "When Wordy Gerdy writes, she rewrites reality itself."

"Don't listen!" Gerdy begged. "Gerdy didn't change! Gerdy stayed things the same!"

"Wordy Gerdy has rewritten your family's stories, one by one. She turned your father into a rabbit … your mother is no bigger than a folded handkerchief … elephants and socks!" Skeleton Keys continued. "Ghost writers do not care to reveal themselves, Kasper – Wordy Gerdy was sure to make her changes so well written that your mind is clouded to the true story. But Ol' Mr Keys knows a *plot hole* when he sees one…"

"Plot hole? Not hole!" Wordy Gerdy shrieked. "Didn't do it!"

Skeleton Keys swept across the kitchen to the fridge. It was covered in photographs, secured with fruit-shaped magnets. The skeleton slipped a photograph from under a magnetic strawberry and held it out to Kasper. "Behold, your *real* family."

Kasper peered at the picture. There he was in the centre, smiling widely, and surrounded by a man, a woman and three more children.

"Didn't do it!" Gerdy squealed.

"M-my family…"
said Kasper, the
realization slapping
him in the face like a
wet fish. He glanced back
at the strange collection of
creatures at the table. "I *remember*."

"CARROTS!" declared the rabbit.

"Stop! Not real! *This* real!" Wordy Gerdy
cried, swooping across the room and
snatching the photograph from Skeleton
Keys' bony hand. She came to a halt in front

27

of the fridge and began tearing off the photographs. "Don't look!"

"Wordy Gerdy, no sooner were you unimagined than you began transforming this poor family into a bunch of who-knows-whatlies," declared Skeleton Keys. "Well, Ol' Mr Keys is here to tell you, you have no right to rewrite – cease your mad modifications this instant!"

Wordy Gerdy turned slowly and glowered at the skeleton.

"No. Gerdy does what Gerdy does – Gerdy *writes*," she hissed. "Gerdy writes you!"

With that, Wordy Gerdy drew her pen swiftly through the air, dragging streaks of green light with each stroke. Up, down, looping and dashing, as if writing on some invisible canvas. In a moment, she had written a word in the air.

The word read 'TOMATO'.

MATO

"Naïve creature, Ol'
Mr Keys is far too *wordy
wise* to be rewritten by
an unruly unimaginary!"
declared Skeleton Keys,
failing to notice that he
suddenly had a bright red tomato in place of a
head. "No revision you envision will affect me!
Now surrender that paranormal pen at once!"

"Never! Gerdy writes! It is what Gerdy does
... it is what Gerdy *is*," Gerdy cried again, her
pen darting left and right, round and round.
"Gerdy will rewrite *everything*."

"Daisy, I do believe that is your cue," said
Skeleton Keys. "Now!"

CHAPTER THREE

THE PEN

(WORDY GERDY'S UNDOING)

Once bitten, Twice Rewritten!

In an instant, the fridge door swung open, smacking straight into Wordy Gerdy with an almighty SLAMM!

"Ooooff!" grunted Wordy Gerdy as she crashed into a nearby cupboard, her pen flying from her hand and skittering across the floor.

"Time's up, *ghoul-girl* – pens down," said a voice as Kasper huddled around the table with his family. He watched in horror as a peculiar figure appeared out of thin air. She looked like a girl of about six, with pigtails, a striped dress and an impish, lopsided grin. Absolutely everything about Daisy was grey, as if she had escaped from a black-and-white photograph.

And her head was on back to front.

"May I present my unimaginary partner-in-problem-solving, Daisy," said Skeleton Keys, spitting out tomato seeds as he spoke. He gave a key-tipped thumbs up to the girl with the backwards head. "Fantabulant work, Daisy. I do believe I am coming around to your dramatic, last-minute entrances!"

"And I'm getting used to saving your useless bones," sneered Daisy, rolling her eyes at the obliviously tomato-headed Skeleton Keys. Then, with an awkward twist, she picked up Wordy Gerdy's pen from the floor. "I'm keeping this, by the way."

"Pen...? Pen!" howled Wordy Gerdy, dazedly rubbing her fridge-flattened face.

"Shut up," Daisy replied, brandishing the pen. "You might be a match for *Mr Tomato-*

head here but I can see right through your rewrites. Why? Because I'm Daisy, that's why. There's no one like me. I'm bad behaviour with a backwards head, and if you mess with me I'll shove this pen so far up your nose you'll smell it in your brain."

"Bad girl! Give pen!" Wordy Gerdy cried out in panic. With a shriek, she flung herself at Daisy, a mad look in her eye.

"I'll show you who's bad, you—" was all Daisy had time to say before Wordy Gerdy collided with her, sending the pen flying once more.

"Got it!" said Skeleton Keys, snatching the pen as it spiralled through the air. "Well flung, Daisy."

"CARROTS!" cried Kasper's dad as Kasper ducked under the table.

"Get off, you grotty ghost," Daisy snarled, giving Wordy Gerdy a shove. The ghostly girl floated into the air, her eyes darting about for her pen.

"Wordy Gerdy, you scammering do-no-good – missing something?" the skeleton cried, waving the pen as he edged towards the back door.

"Pen! Gerdy needs!" Wordy Gerdy howled as thunder struck again.

Skeleton Keys thrust his left thumb into the keyhole. With a CLICK CLUNK he pulled the door ajar and held out the pen. "Come no closer, for I have opened a door to a secret place only I know!"

"Place? What place?" Gerdy asked.

"If I told you it would not be secret, now would it?" tutted the skeleton, his tomato head lolling from side to side. "Undo your rewrites and restore reality, Wordy Gerdy. If you do not undo, it will be your undoing, for I shall fling this pen into who-knows-where, and you shall never see it again!"

"No! Not pen, Gerdy needs!" shrieked Wordy Gerdy. "Gerdy will undo!" With that, she stuck her fingers in her ears and puffed out her cheeks. Everyone froze.

A moment later, there came a

POP

– and everything changed.

CHAPTER FOUR

TIME'S UP

(HOW DO YOU SOLVE A PROBLEM
LIKE WORDY GERDY?)

"Ten keys are better than one!"
—*SK*

The echoing POP was not like a soap bubble or even a balloon ... this was the sound of *everything* popping – of reality itself popping back into shape.

"I can taste ... carrots," said a voice. Kasper turned to see his dad, no longer an enormous rabbit. The rest of his family were similarly restored – Kasper's mother towered over him as well she should and his brothers and sisters were as human as you might expect.

"Much better," said Skeleton Keys, blissfully unaware that his tomato head was a skull once more.

"Mr Bones give pen!" Wordy Gerdy wailed. "Mr Bones promised!" She screamed as Skeleton Keys flung the door wide.

"You want this pen, rugslugger? Go and fetch it!" said the skeleton. With that, he tossed Wordy Gerdy's pen out of the doorway. The ghostly girl swooped straight past the skeleton and pursued the pen outside with a desperate howl.

"And that," added Skeleton Keys, "is how you solve a problem like Wordy Gerdy."

"I'm sorry!" cried Kasper, running into his parents' arms with tears in his eyes. "I-I didn't mean to imagine her..."

"Imagine who?" said Kasper's big brother. As Kasper looked up at him, it was already hard to imagine he was once a sock puppet.

"Do not blame yourself, Kasper – imaginations are flabbergasting at the best of times," explained Skeleton Keys, glancing out of the door. "Some unimaginaries are simply too wild, too unruly, too rottering ... they do not understand that the world beyond the imagined has *rules*."

"Well, I thought they were better as rabbits and socks," huffed Daisy. She peered out through the open door. The first thing she noticed was that it was not a stormy night outside. In fact, it was no longer night at all, nor was there any sign of the city. Instead, Daisy saw a green forest in bright daylight. Leafy trees jutted from a thick blanket of grey-white fog, and Wordy Gerdy appeared and disappeared from the mist, frantically searching the forest floor for her lost pen.

"So, where did you send her?" Daisy asked.

"Wordy Gerdy's villainy is a thing of the past – literally," Skeleton Keys explained, pulling his key-tipped thumb out of the lock and wiggling it in Daisy's face. "For this is *the Key to Time*."

"Ugh, I hate when you do time travel, it always goes wrong," said Daisy.

"Pifflechips! I have sent Wordy Gerdy into the distant past," he replied, turning away from the door. "Now the rampant rewriter has a couple of centuries to think about what she has done. Ol' Mr Keys does it again – everything has gone according to my untestable plan!"

"Uh, excuse me..." Kasper said, staring out of the door.

"Plan? Pfff, you were getting tomato-headed *nowhere* before I turned up to save the day, you useless bag of bones," replied Daisy. "I don't know how you coped so long without me."

"*Excuse* me..." Kasper said again.

"Puffwinkles!" continued Skeleton Keys. "Need I remind you, I was dealing with errant unimaginaries before you were so much as a twinkle in a mind's eye. For you see, with these ten remarkable keys and a healthy dollop of fabulush fantabulance, there is nothing that cannot be—"

"Excuse me!"

Skeleton Keys turned to Kasper. The boy's arm was outstretched as he pointed a trembling finger towards the back door. Skeleton Keys and Daisy turned.

Wordy Gerdy floated, still and silent, above the blanket of fog.

And she was holding her pen.

"Found it…" Wordy Gerdy said in a strange, sing-song tone, and began to drag her pen through the air once more.

"Shut the door, *now*," Daisy snapped, but it was too late – Wordy Gerdy's pen arced through the air as swiftly as a sword, up and down, round and round, streaking through the air as it lit up the sky with a single word.

The word read 'KEYS'.

"Have you learned nothing, unimaginary? Your pen has no power over me – not as long as I have these nine keys to protect me!" Skeleton Keys scoffed, admiring his key-tipped fingers. Then he grabbed the door handle and began to push it closed. "I am sorry, but your time is well and truly—"

"Wait," interrupted Daisy, jamming her foot in the doorway. "Did you say *nine* keys?"

CHAPTER FIVE

PAST, TENSE

(HAS ANYONE SEEN MY KEYS?)

Travels in time are a tricky affair
When where becomes when,
and when becomes where!
But stick to this rule and stick to it fast
NEVER BUMP INTO YOUR OWN PAST

"Nine keys? Flabberjabs," replied Skeleton Keys, wiggling his fingers proudly. "I have always had *seven* remarkable keys. Here they are, for the counting..."

Daisy peered at the skeleton's bone digits. The keys on his left hand were present and accounted for, but his right hand had no keys at all. It was as if they were never there.

"Seven? You're down to five keys, dummy," she said.

"Five?" said Skeleton Keys, inspecting his fingers. "But I have never had more than *four* keys, look!"

Sure enough, another key had vanished.

"You stupid bag of bones, it's *her*," snapped Daisy. "She's writing your keys out of your story..."

"Gerdy...?" said Kasper. He glanced out of the back door again to see Wordy Gerdy hovering above the forest floor, a victorious grin spreading across her face.

Daisy fixed her glare upon the key at the end of Skeleton Key's left index finger. Suddenly, it was just a finger. The key was gone, as if it was never there.

"Stupid skeleton, you don't even see it, do you?"

"Both of my keys are just fine, thank you very much," said Skeleton Keys, admiring his two remaining key-tipped fingers as if nothing was untoward. Before his very eyes, another key vanished. "I do not think we shall have any more surprises today. Not as long as I have my wonderfilling, one-and-only key…"

Skeleton Keys gave Daisy a thumbs up and she watched in horror as the final key, *the Key to Time*, began to fade out of existence. And as it faded, so did the portal into the past.

"Ugh, *time travel* is always more trouble than it's worth," Daisy snarled. "You owe me for this, bone-bag…"

"For what?" said Skeleton Keys. "What are you t— AAH!"

Daisy shoved Skeleton Keys as hard as she could, and they both stumbled through the doorway. A moment later, the skeleton's final key vanished from existence and, with it, the portal between the present and past.

They landed in a crumpled heap between two trees.

"Pen belongs to Gerdy!" cried Wordy Gerdy with a breathy cackle. "Gerdy writes! Gerdy writes everything!"

Daisy pulled herself slowly to her feet, mad rage burning in her strange grey eyes. "Give me that pen, or I'll turn your head the same way as mine and *really* give you something to cry about."

"Aah! Not take! Not pen!" wailed the ghoulish unimaginary.

With that, Gerdy darted through the air,
weaving between trees before vanishing into
the fog.

"Get back here, so I can shove that pen up
your nose!" Daisy shouted as Skeleton Keys
suddenly loomed behind her.

"Daisy!" he barked, dusting himself off
with his bone fingers. "I am well aware you
crave a level of lunacy that anyone else would
consider bad for the humours, but this must
be your most confuddling behaviour to date!

What were you thinking?"

"What were *you* thinking?" Daisy sneered. "You didn't even see Wordy Gerdy coming. She rewrote your story and you didn't even realize."

"Popdimples! I think I would know if Wordy Gerdy had rewritten the tale of Ol' Mr Keys," said the skeleton.

Daisy let out a growl and grabbed his hands. "The things you *should* know but don't could fill a swimming pool, bone-bag," she tutted, holding his keyless fingers up in front of his face. *"She. Took. Your. Keys."*

"What keys?" asked the skeleton.

"Argh!" Daisy snapped, flinging her arms in the air. "What was I thinking, wasting my time with a broken-brained bag of bones? I should have ditched you months ago. You sent ghoul-girl back in time and then *left the door open.* If I hadn't shoved us through the doorway you would have lost your only chance of getting your keys back. I can't be stuck two hundred years ago, I've got things to do and people to torment..."

"Fret not, Daisy. If Wordy Gerdy has indeed rewritten my story, I can assure you I am no less impressive for it," declared Skeleton Keys. "If what you are telling me is correct, that rugslugging rewriter has managed to write my *knees* out of existence."

"Keys, not knees, you dummy," groaned Daisy.

"Precisely," Skeleton Keys continued. "So, all we need to do is find Wordy Gerdy here in the past and seize her paranormal pen once more. She will have no choice but to undo her maddening modifications, thus restoring my trees!"

"Keys!" Daisy growled.

"Exactly!" said the skeleton. "Then we can banish her pesky pen once and for all and return forthwith to the present, complete with my fantabulant— I want to say *peas...*"

"Keys! Why would you want— Of course not peas! Keys! Keys!" Daisy yelled. Then she took a deep breath and straightened her dress. "OK, *fine*. Let's find *Pen E. Dreadful* and steal her silly pen. Ugh, it's going to be like looking for a ghost in a haystack in this fog..."

Skeleton Keys turned his head with a dry creak.

"Perhaps not," he said, peering out beyond the forest. The fog stretched out over a patchwork of rolling, grassy fields dotted with trees until, in the far distance, it met the city. It was far smaller than the one

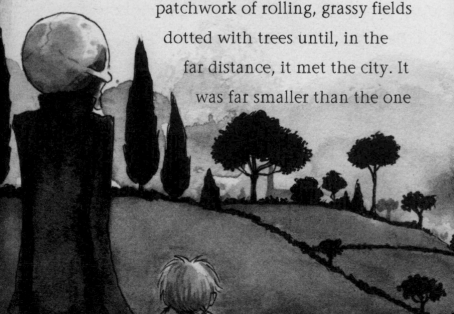

they had left in the present – an ominous, dark shadow of a place that coughed up thick, sky-darkening plumes of charcoal smoke.

"There," he said, pointing a keyless finger towards the smoke. "Wordy Gerdy lives to rewrite reality – she will go where the stories are."

"Looks like the sort of place I could start trouble – let's go," said Daisy.

"Indeed, let us not diddle-dally! We will get my lost cheese back in no time!"

"It's ke— Ugh, *forget it*," groaned Daisy.

CHAPTER SIX

INTO THE CITY

(IN THE SHAPE OF A KEY)

If you come 'ome to find a key
Is carved upon your door
Step inside and you will find
That 'ome is 'ome no more!

Your every trinket, coin and gem
Has upped and walked away
To find another 'ome! For that
Is city life today!

The sun was beginning its slow descent to the horizon when Skeleton Keys and Daisy arrived in the city. The wide, fog-lined streets were thronged with busy, purposeful townsfolk and large, grand horse-cabs rumbling this way and that. The whole place was filled with clamour and noise. As the decidedly conspicuous pair ventured further and the crowds grew denser, Daisy played her usual trick of turning invisible.

"Why is everyone dressed like you?" she asked, glancing around at the townsfolk in tailored tailcoats and finely embroidered dresses. "And why does everything smell like horse poo and un-flushed toilets?"

"Why, this is the fine-stink and flowery end of town – you should get a noseful of the *rookeries*," explained Skeleton Keys. "Those not born into the shine of favour have been driven yonder to a ramshackling maze of narrow alleyways and crumbledown houses, cram-bursting with fellow-me-folks born to a life of less."

"You sound like you've been here before," Daisy said. "You'd suit a smelly dump like this."

"Been ... before?" Skeleton Keys mused. He suddenly stopped in the middle of the street as if struck squarely in the face by a distant memory. The skeleton looked back, then forwards. Left, then right.

"Crumcrinkles, it cannot be!" he whispered.

He suddenly ducked down a side street and hurried up to the door of a rather grand-looking townhouse.

"What are you doing, dummy?" sighed the still-invisible Daisy, hurrying after him as fast she could with a back-to-front head.

The skeleton raced to the next house along and inspected its door with dismay.

"Dogs 'n' cats!" he hissed, darting to the next house. Then to the next and the next, checking each door in turn. "Sticks 'n' stones! Horse 'n' cart! Cheese 'n' biscuits!"

"Silly skeleton … *slow down*," Daisy puffed, racing after Skeleton Keys with a look of fury fixed to her face. "What is wrong with you?"

"Everything is wrong! We must away!" hissed Skeleton Keys, racing up to one more door and pointing at it.

"Away? We just got here," said Daisy.

"By my bones, what have I done? We cannot be here! *I* cannot be here!" said the skeleton, pointing at the door. "*Look.*"

Daisy squinted. A shape had been crudely carved into the wood.

It was a *key.*

"Curse that foul phantom, she left my mind all soupy 'n' slop-about!" the skeleton added, darting behind a nearby lamppost to hide. "I should have realized where I was ... *when* I was."

"What are you on about? What's the deal with those keys?"

"It was her! She carved them on the doors, in honour of her imaginary friend..."

"*Her?* Her who?"

Skeleton Keys looked strange all of a sudden. Paler, as if such a thing was possible.

Then he spoke a single word – a *name*. And from the way he said it, Daisy knew that name meant more to Skeleton Keys than anything.

"*Emily.*"

CHAPTER SEVEN

EMILY

(THE UNTOLD STORY OF SKELETON KEYS)

*It is a truth universally acknowledged, that a
singular mind with a wild imagination can work
unimaginable wonders!*

"Emily..." Skeleton Keys said again, poking his head out from behind the lamppost. He looked suddenly lost – transported from the present by memories of the past.

"Who's Emily?" asked Daisy, reappearing. "Keep it short, I get bored easily."

"Emily is – *was* – the reason for my being," Skeleton Keys replied. "The reason I exist ... the reason for Ol' Mr Keys! It was Emily who *imagined* me."

Daisy had never heard Skeleton Keys mention *anyone* from his past before. She suddenly felt oddly flustered. "So what?"

"For a time, I was but a figment of her wild imagining," replied Skeleton Keys. "Then, all of a suddenly, she imagined me so wildly and so well, that I became as real as heartbeats. Emily made me unimaginary."

"This story is already going on too long," Daisy groaned. "Then what happened?"

"Why, *everything* happened!" declared Skeleton Keys. "Emily was everything *I* had ever imagined a friend could be. She was … flabbergasting! As fine and fantabulant a ringdinger as it is possible to imagine. And *I* was precisely what Emily had imagined."

"A silly skeleton?" replied Daisy.

"Not just any skeleton. I had … had…" Skeleton Keys muttered, peering down at his fingers. "Keys! Why, I had the most flabbergasting keys, Daisy! Do you not remember?"

"That's exactly what I've been trying to tell you, you stupid—"

"Ten remarkable keys, Daisy! How could you have forgotten?" said the skeleton in a reverie. "With them, I could open doors to hidden worlds and secret places ... take Emily wherever she wanted. We could go anywhere and beyond, and that is exactly what we did! Every door we opened led to another adventure – a hundred wonderfilling worlds that even the wildest imagination could not invent. Emily faced the unknown and the unknowable as if it was her destiny. She met the living, the dead and everything in between – the imaginary and the unimaginary. But it was I who benefited most – for Emily showed me how to be brave and adventuresome and kind and hopeful – to be human, in all its fine fantabulance. She vowed that we would dedicate ourselves to protecting those with wild imaginations, and to keeping a watchful eye over the newly unimagined."

"She sounds too goody two shoes to be true," noted Daisy.

"So many unimaginaries, so many adventures," Skeleton Keys continued. "Though I barely noticed, time passed. Years went by ... decades disappeared in a blur of adventure. With so many worlds and wild imaginings, I did not see what was happening right in front of my eye sockets – I did not notice Emily growing *old*. Before I knew it, her story was nearing its end. I could not imagine spending a single day – a single *moment* without her. Wherever Emily was going, I wanted to go too ... but I could not. 'All that matters now is the future – *never bump into your own past*,' she said. Emily told me that it was up to me to protect those with wild imaginations, whenever and wherever I was needed. And then ... she was gone. Ol' Mr Keys was alone."

For a long moment, there was silence.

"And?" said Daisy impatiently.

"To be separated from Emily was almost too much to bear," Skeleton Keys said at last. "To live those days again – to live even one more day with Emily would be the greatest day of all."

Daisy reached her arms behind her back and rubbed her eyes. "Let me get this straight. You sent ghoul-girl back in time to your own past ... back to your own *plotline*? Why not just send her back to the land of the dinosaurs?"

"It was the first time I thought of!" admitted Skeleton Keys. "When I think of the past, *this* is the past I think of."

"Ugh, I didn't think it was possible but you're even more bone-headed than you look," Daisy groaned. "Anyway, what has any of this got to do with getting us home?"

"Do you not see? My very presence here is *dangerous!*" the skeleton replied. "Never bump into your own past, Emily said – it is the first rule of time travel! And also rules two to eleven. She was very clear – even a chance meeting or greeting with my past – with *her* – and the universe will sneeze itself out of existence! The End of Everything!"

"That sounds silly, even for you," said Daisy.

"Cheese 'n' biscuits, we must get away from this city as quick-sharpish as possible, before—"

"But you said ghoul-girl was here!"

"Are you not listening, Daisy? The End. Of. *Everything*. We must flee this place forthwith!"

"NO." Daisy turned to the skeleton with that mad look in her eye. "You listen to me, bone-head. We're not leaving here 'til we get your keys back. We're going to find ghoul-girl and

make her undo her
doings, and then I'm
going to break that pen
over her silly head. And
then you're going to send
us back when we belong

... or at least to a place where
everything doesn't smell like horse poo."

"But—" began Skeleton Keys.

"Because if I end up stuck in the past, I am
going to *find* your precious Emily," added
Daisy, "and I'm going to make sure her life is
one hundred per cent rubbish. I'll make her
wish she never imagined you in the first place
... I'll make her wish she'd never been *born*."

Skeleton Keys paused for a moment as Daisy
glowered at him.

"A compelling argument," he said at last.
"Very well, let us find ourselves a ghost
writer."

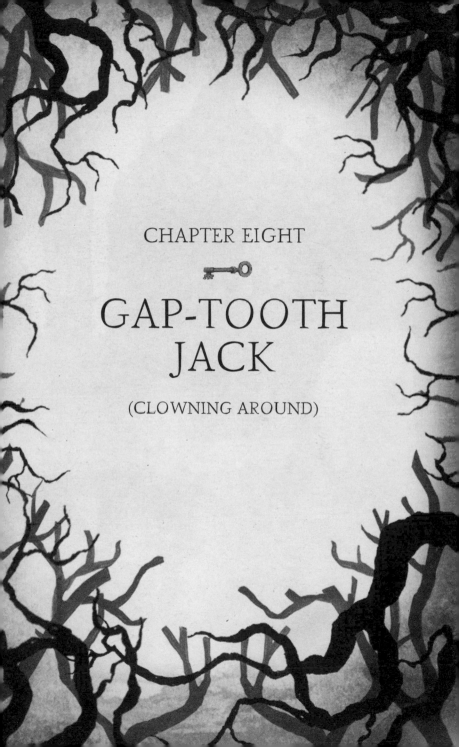

CHAPTER EIGHT

GAP-TOOTH JACK

(CLOWNING AROUND)

No pocket's safe, no lock secure
From the wily, smiley entrepreneur
What e'er he takes, he'll not give back
He's grubby, grinnin' Gap-tooth Jack!

"So, where do we look for *Mary, Mary, Thinks She's Scary?*" Daisy asked as she followed Skeleton Keys through the city in search of Wordy Gerdy.

"Ghost writers go where there are stories to be told, or re-told," the skeleton replied, his eyes darting nervously around for any sign of the girl who imagined him. He slipped down an alleyway, snaking through the shadows with long, silent strides until he arrived at a bustling town square. It was surrounded on all sides by tall buildings peppered with grim, stone gargoyles. In the middle of the square stood an impressive wooden clock tower with a high spire, while around its edges were shops and market stalls, selling bread, flowers, fruit, sweets and clothing.

"I must remain *undercovered* – the merest brush with my own past could flush everything down the toilet of reality. Happily, I still have a trick or two in my top pocket..." said the skeleton. He reached a bony hand into a small pocket in his tailcoat and pulled on what looked like the tip of a black silk handkerchief. He pulled and pulled until he had drawn out a scarf as long as his arm and then wrapped it around his head until his skull was all but concealed.

"How do I look?" he asked. Only the skeleton's glowering white eyes could be seen beneath his disguise.

"No stupider than usual," said Daisy.

"Give the square a scout 'n' about, Daisy," he said. "Wordy Gerdy should be drawn to crowds like flies are drawn to muckery. She will want as many stories as possible upon which to practise her penmanship. I will remain hidden here, lest I bump into you-know-who, and Everything Ends."

"So, I'm left doing your dirty work again?" Daisy groaned. "It's not just the horses that *stink* around here..."

"And *please*, Daisy, for the sake of the universe itself, try to keep a low profile."

With a tut, Daisy left Skeleton Keys to slink deeper into the shadows of the alleyway and made her way to the square. She passed the door to a sweet shop and made a mental note to rob the place before they returned to the present; for now, she turned invisible and clambered up on to a fruit stall to get a better look. Had the fruit seller not been busy arranging her oranges, she might have seen a single apple appear to float into the air of its own accord.

I'm going to stick that ghost's pen in her ear and write my name on her brain, Daisy thought, munching the apple to its core in a few angry bites.

Ahead of her, a large, noisy crowd had gathered in a semicircle beneath the clock tower to watch a street performer. He was a round man dressed in a blousy white outfit with a frilly collar and oversized buttons. On his head he wore a wig comprising three tufts of shaggy hair, and his face was covered in white make-up. He delighted the townsfolk with tricks and tomfoolery as they threw coins into a hat lying at his feet.

"What a clown," scoffed Daisy, watching

the man kick himself in the backside to wild
applause. She peered up at the surrounding
buildings, hoping to catch even the faintest
ghostly glow. With a *"Huh?"* she narrowed
her eyes. High above her, she saw a small,
swift figure hurrying along the rooftops on
one side of the square. The figure suddenly
stopped atop a roaring, lion-headed gargoyle
and unspooled a length of rope, before
flinging its looped end into the air. Almost
impossibly, the rope flew gracefully across the
square and the loop hooked around the clock
tower's spire. The figure immediately leaped
off the roof, swinging unseen above the heads
of the townsfolk. Daisy felt her jaw fall open
as the swooping stranger let go of the rope at
the last moment and landed stylishly at the
clown's feet.

"Evenin', Funnyface!" cried the stranger,
scooping up the clown's money-filled hat

in an instant. "And thank you for your kind
donation!"

"*You* again!" the clown gasped. He threw
a punch but the nimble thief ducked and,
faster than a ferret, scampered under the
clown's legs and then up on to his back. "Get
off me!" the clown cried as the thief climbed
on to his shoulders and flashed a smile that
showed a gap where two front teeth should
have been.

"Why, it's him!" cried someone in the
crowd. "It's Gap-tooth JACK!"

"Show's over, folks, and I'll be your
encore!" laughed the pickpocket, balancing
on the clown's shoulders just long
enough for Daisy to get a good look

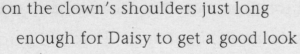

from her perch at the back of the crowd.

Gap-tooth Jack was no older than ten, and *impossibly* filthy. His face was so caked in grime, dirt and soot as to make him barely recognizable as human. He was so grubby that a flying beetle buzzed around his head, presumably tempted by the unwashed wafts that the boy gave off. Gap-tooth Jack wore ragged clothes, a flat cap pulled low over his brow and shoes so worn that his toes poked out from the ends.

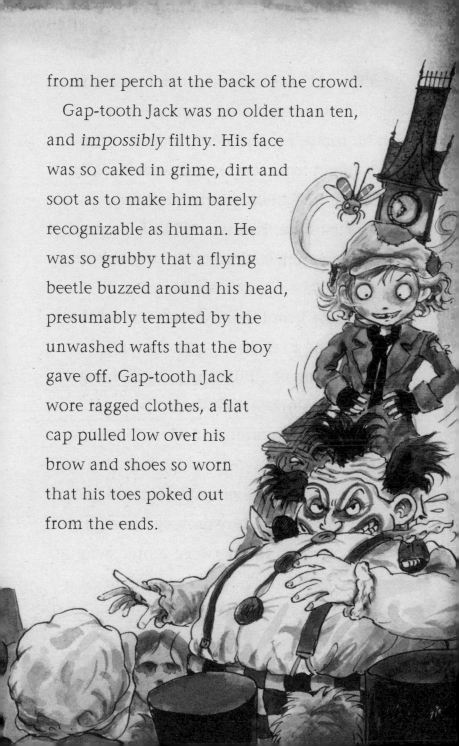

"Off, I say!" the clown roared, thrashing wildly. In the end, all he managed to do was hit himself in the head, as Gap-tooth Jack vaulted from the clown's shoulders and landed on the cobbles with a deft roll.

"'Til next time, Funnyface!" Jack laughed, before vanishing back into the bewildered crowd with the clown's hat full of loot.

"My name is *not* 'Funnyface'!" roared the clown, trying to push his way through the throng in pursuit. "Pilfering pest, I'll hang you from a lamppost! I'll drown you in a puddle! I'll bake you in a pie!"

Daisy hopped down from the fruit stall. From the back of the crowd, she could just about make out the boy moving like a gust of wind, under legs and between limbs, swiping yet more cash from pockets as he went. She could not help but be impressed. "Little *thief*," she noted as Gap-tooth Jack darted out from the crowd, the buzzing beetle hot on his heels. In fact, Daisy was so distracted by the boy who was now racing straight towards her, she altogether forgot that she was invisible.

A moment later, Gap-tooth Jack ran into her – and into more trouble than he'd ever known.

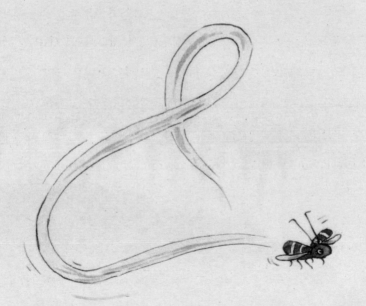

CHAPTER NINE

FUNNYFACE

(WORDY GERDY'S NEW BEST FRIEND)

"Your pocket is my destination
Thank you for your kind donation!"
—Gap-tooth Jack

"Uff-uff!" Gap-tooth Jack grunted as he and Daisy both tumbled to the ground. The clown's stolen hat flew from the boy's hand, scattering coins across the cobbles. Daisy, meanwhile, was so surprised by the collision that she didn't even realize she was no longer invisible. By the time she sat up, Jack was staring her straight in the eye.

"Where'd you spring from?" Jack asked with a grin. He immediately grabbed Daisy by the arm and dragged her with him as he ducked for cover behind the fruit stall.

"You should watch where you're going," tutted Daisy, pulling away.

"Sorry about that – I could have sworn you weren't there a second ago," whispered Jack. "Also, you might need to see a doctor – I think I knocked your head the wrong way round."

"Actually, I was unimagined this way," Daisy replied proudly.

"Unimagined?" Jack repeated as the buzzing beetle landed on top of his cap. "You mean, like Chuckaboo here? That's a turn-up – me and Chuck figured he was the only one. Whose imagination did you spring from, then?"

"Mind your own business," Daisy replied. "And I'm pretty sure your beetle's just a plain old beetle. I'm looking for a *proper* unimaginary – a see-through girl with a magic pen. Have you seen her?"

"Magic pen? I could do with one of those,"

replied Jack, looking for an opportune time to escape the square. "While I wrack my memory, would you mind checking if there's a clown around? I'm sort of in his bad books."

"Ugh, fine, but you have to show me how to do stealing," Daisy huffed, poking her head over the stall. "Then I'm going to steal ghoul-girl's pen and stick it in— *Huh*?"

Daisy narrowed her eyes as she glanced up over the heads of the crowd and up to the clock tower. Its spire seemed to be giving off a faint greenish glow.

Then she saw her.

Hovering high above the crowd in front of the clock face, gazing down at the crowd with pen in hand, was none other than Wordy Gerdy.

"Well, well, old bone-bag was right," she hissed. "If it isn't *Penderella*."

"I don't mean to be a bother," whispered

Gap-tooth Jack, tugging at Daisy's dress. "But is there any sign of—"

"GOTCHA."

As quick as a flash, a hand reached over the top of the fruit stall and grabbed Gap-tooth Jack by the collar of his jacket.

The clown had found him.

"No escape for you this time, boy!" he growled, hoisting Gap-tooth Jack into the air. "I'll pull out the teeth you have left, see how you like thieving then!"

"Lemme down! Didn't your mother teach you not to pick on a poor, defenceless child?" Jack protested as the beetle buzzed angrily around the clown's head.

For a moment Daisy considered trying to help the thief – especially since she'd failed to notice the clown sneaking up on them – but then she looked back up at the clock tower. Wordy Gerdy slowly circled the spire, her pen twitching in her hand as she decided whose reality to rewrite first. Daisy glanced back at the alleyway but there was no sign of Skeleton Keys. A lopsided grin spread across her face.

"Time you were *grounded*, Floaty McFloatface." She grabbed another apple from the fruit stall and strode out from behind it. Then, with an awkward spin, she flung the apple as hard as she could into the air. It flew towards the clock tower.

With a

DONK

the apple landed, uncannily, between
Wordy Gerdy's eyes. She let out a yelp
and plummeted down into the crowd. The
townsfolk immediately began to scatter in
panic at the sight of this strange, glowing girl
who fell from the sky.

"*Bullseye,*" said Daisy. Leaving Gap-tooth
Jack as he tried in vain to break free of the
clown's grip, the girl with the backwards
head began ambling towards the stunned
unimaginary lying on the cobbles. "Bone-bag
needs his keys back, ghoul-girl," Daisy said.
"You don't 'pop' everything back to normal
in the next five seconds, I'm going to make
you eat that pen for dinner."

Wordy Gerdy didn't move. Daisy paused

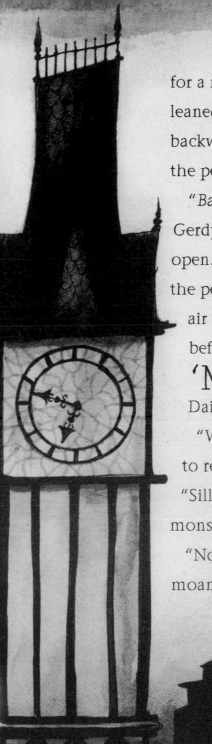

for a moment and then leaned over her, craning her backwards-facing body to grab the pen.

"*Bad* girl," said Wordy Gerdy, her eyes suddenly open. In an instant, she swirled the pen quickly through the air and a word appeared before her eyes.

'MONSTER'.

Daisy stopped in her tracks.

"Wait, are you trying to rewrite me?" she said.

"Silly ghost – I'm *already* a monster."

"Not you, bad girl," Gerdy moaned. "*Him*."

Daisy slowly turned. The clown, still wrestling with the squirming Gap-tooth Jack, let out a sudden, blood-curdling howl. He began thrashing wildly about, so much so that Gap-tooth Jack managed to slip out of his own jacket. As Jack dropped to the cobbles, the clown began to *change*. With a crunch of bones and the wrenching of muscle, he doubled in size in an instant.

In moments, the clown was transformed into a hunched, beastly ogre – a monster of a man, with vast, ape-like arms. The red hair of his wig had become a huge, three-crested mane, and more scarlet fur sprouted from his body through rips in his costume. Daisy saw a gaping grin appear upon the clown's face, pushing the rest of his features aside.

"Funnyface is on
Gerdy's side now,"
said Wordy Gerdy as
the monstrous clown
turned to face Daisy.
"Funnyface is
Gerdy's new
best friend."

CHAPTER TEN

GET GAP-TOOTH JACK!

(THE CLOCK TOWER FALLS)

"Catch me if you can, snare me if you dare!"
—Gap-tooth Jack

As bystanders fled screaming at the sight of the clown monster, he stomped towards Daisy and loomed over her, his grin fixed and taut, drool dripping slowly between his teeth.

Daisy held her nose.

"You need to brush your teeth," she said as the monster's hot breath stung her eyes. "You smell worse than everything else around here, and everything else around here stinks."

Daisy didn't even see Funnyface's great, clawed hand coming. He wrapped it around

her and hoisted her into the air, squeezing her
so tightly that she couldn't even concentrate
enough to turn invisible.

"Hold her tight, while Gerdy writes!" said
Gerdy, floating triumphantly back into the
air. "No one takes pen! Gerdy will teach you.
Gerdy will turn bad girl into an *apple...*"

Wordy Gerdy held her pen in front of
Daisy's face – except it suddenly wasn't there.
Her hand was empty.

"P-pen?" she shrieked, looking around.
"Where is *pen?*"

"What, you mean *this* pen?" said a voice.
Gerdy spun round in the air. As the last of
the panicking crowd fled the square, there,
standing firm, was Gap-tooth Jack.

And he was holding Wordy Gerdy's pen.

"PEN!"

Wordy Gerdy's cry echoed around the
square.

"Catch me if you can, snare me if you dare!" cried Gap-tooth Jack. He raced towards the clock tower and immediately began scaling it with breathtaking agility.

"Funnyface! Get pen! Bring stinker *down*," howled Wordy Gerdy.

At her command, the grinning monster dropped Daisy on to the cobbles and strode towards the clock tower with thunderous steps. He wasted no time in wrapping his great arms around the base of the tower. Incredible muscles strained as Funnyface pulled with all his might.

Gap-tooth Jack climbed higher, his beetle buzzing frantically around his head. He heard the creak and crack of splintering wood as the tower began to shudder and sway. Then, with a single almighty heave, the monster wrenched the entire structure from its foundations.

Below, a dazed Daisy sat up, just as a dark
shadow fell over her – the tower was falling.
She looked up and saw the clock face racing
towards her. There was no way she could get
clear in time...

"Daisy!"

No sooner had Daisy heard Skeleton Keys'
cry, than she felt bony hands scoop her off
the ground.

An instant later, a ground-shuddering
KRASSH filled the air as the tower
smashed on to the cobbles.

"Low – *oww* – profile, I said," Skeleton
Keys groaned as they lay in a crumpled
heap, inches from the wreckage of the tower.

Thick clouds of choking dust filled the air.

"What – *koff* – is that supposed to mean?" Daisy wheezed.

"I mean, is there no situation into which you cannot inject chaos and calamity?" replied the skeleton.

"I didn't do anything!" Daisy protested. "And, while we're on the subject, neither did you! Did you not see the *giant clown monster*?"

"I was in hiding, for the sake of the universe!" said Skeleton Keys. "Daisy, could you not, for once, focus on the catastrophe in hand, instead of creating more? We must find Wordy Gerdy and retrieve her pen so that—"

"Funnyface! Find Gerdy's pen!"

"By my bones, I hear her!" Skeleton Keys said at the cry. "Pay attention, Daisy – Wordy Gerdy is close."

"*Obviously,*" Daisy groaned, casting her gaze through the dust across the square. She could see Wordy Gerdy and her clown monster, already scouring the wreckage of the clock tower, but there was no sign of Gap-tooth Jack – that is, until she spotted a familiar beetle fly over the wreckage to an alleyway on the other side of the square. There, unfeasibly unscathed and twirling Wordy Gerdy's pen around his fingers, was Gap-tooth Jack.

"He's got it ... he's *got the pen,*" said Daisy as the beetle came to rest atop the thief's head.

"Who?"

"Gap-tooth Jack!"

"Blacktooth who?" repeated the skeleton.

"Gap-tooth— It doesn't matter! He stole ghoul-girl's pen!" said Daisy, pointing to the alley as Gap-tooth Jack darted away. "We can take it from *him* instead of having to fight ghoul-girl's smelly-breath monster. Come on..."

"Wait! All our efforts to retrieve the pen will be in vain if I bump into Emily and the universe explodes," explained the skeleton. "We must wait for the dead of night, when the city slumbers. Then we can retrieve the pen from this Gumtooth John and Wordy Gerdy will have no choice but to return my keys."

"Night-time is *ages* away," Daisy hissed. "If we let *Happily Gappily* get away now, how will we ever find him?"

"It has been a century or two, but I know this city like the back of my carpal bones," said Skeleton Keys, dusting himself off. "I shall simply follow my nose."

Daisy reached her hand around her back and slapped her palm against her forehead.

"You don't even *have* a nose..."

CHAPTER ELEVEN

SKELETON KEYS FOLLOWS HIS NOSE

(THE TRUTH ABOUT GAP-TOOTH JACK)

He comes, he takes, he goes, that's Jack!
He smiles, he runs, he don't look back!
A flash of tooth, a smart remark
Then gone! A shadow in the dark

Despite Daisy's protestations, Skeleton Keys would not begin his search for Gap-tooth Jack until nightfall. As darkness fell, they set off, making their way into the dingy heart of the city. Wide, lamp-lit roads gave way to narrow, gloomy backstreets. Everywhere Daisy looked, she saw shabby, ramshackle buildings rising higher and higher the further they went, obscuring even the faintest moonlight. Dense fog hung like a shadow and the city's foul smells were replaced with even more intolerable aromas. This was no longer the realm of fine folk – these streets belonged to the lost and forgotten.

"We've been looking for at *least* a million years," Daisy moaned. "Admit it, you have no idea where you're going."

"The rookeries are as dark and confuddling a maze as you will ever find but we are getting close to that pen – I can feel it in my bones," whispered Skeleton Keys, checking his scarf disguise was still wrapped tightly around his head. "But every moment we remain in the city, we run the risk of bursting the universe like an over-inflated balloon. The End of Everything..."

"It'd be a relief – this dump has the smelliest stink so far," said Daisy. With a pointed huff, she added, "I bet your precious *girlfriend* wouldn't be seen dead in a place like this."

"Ah, but Emily's life did not begin as it ended – once upon a tale, she was no more than— Aha!" Skeleton Keys stopped outside a door so bafflingly small that Daisy didn't even notice it until the skeleton leaned low and twisted the handle.

"Here?" asked a dubious Daisy. "That door's hardly big enough for a beetle."

"The nose knows," replied Skeleton Keys. "I bet my bones that the thief is inside. Why, it is almost as though I have been here before…"

With a push, the door creaked dryly open. The skeleton contorted his body until he squeezed through and disappeared into even darker shadows. Daisy ducked and followed him. She emerged inside an ink-black passageway, so dark that she was forced to feel her way along the wall.

"All so confuddlingly familiar…" whispered Skeleton Keys, peering through the darkness up a flight of rickety stairs.

"Stupid nose," huffed Daisy. She pursued the skeleton up the stairs, each creakier than the last, until finally he pushed open a door to a murky attic. Moonlight streaked in through a cracked window at the far end of the room, which was empty but for a single moth-eaten mattress.

Daisy checked the door to find a key in its lock. She turned invisible.

"Greetings ... is anyone there?" called Skeleton Keys, edging into the dingy room. He moved with cautious strides, his eyes adjusting to the darkness.

"Crumcrinkles, I feel like I *know* this place," he whispered. "I suppose it must be my no-oOOOOOOH!"

In an instant, a thick net dragged Skeleton Keys off his feet and pulled tight around him. Before he knew what was happening, he was hoisted into the air.

"What have we got here, Chuckaboo? Another one of that green ghost's beasties, maybe?" said a voice as the skeleton dangled helplessly in the net. From the gloomiest corner of the attic emerged Gap-tooth Jack, his beetle perched happily atop his flat cap, and in his hand, Wordy Gerdy's pen.

"Chuckaboo? Where have I heard that name before...?" said the skeleton, trying to catch a glimpse of Gap-tooth Jack as the net spun slowly around.

"Reckon you'd thieve from a thief, did you?" said Gap-tooth Jack, showily throwing and catching the pen.

"That voice..." said Skeleton Keys. "I *know* that voice..."

"Well, you can tell that ghost that if I steal somethin', it stays stole," Gap-tooth Jack continued. "If you want to catch me by surprise, you've got to get up bright and early..."

"I like to stay up late," said Daisy's voice in the darkness. Jack spun around as the door suddenly slammed shut, seemingly of its own accord.

"Dogs 'n' cats!" Jack cried.

"'Dogs 'n' cats'?" repeated Skeleton Keys,

trying to squeeze his face through the net
to get a better look. "Why, the only folk to
utter that snappy catchphrase are Ol' Mr Keys
and— Oh *no*."

The key in the door turned with a CLICK
CLUNK, before removing itself from the lock
and hanging, suspended, in the air. A moment
later, Daisy materialized, key in hand.

"Boo, guess who," she said with a lopsided
grin.

"You!" Jack cried.

"We need that pen, so give," Daisy replied.
With that, she dropped the key through
a wide crack in the floorboards and it
disappeared into darkness.

"Daisy! Wait!" Skeleton Keys pleaded in his
loudest whisper. "It is her!"

"Stay out of this, bone-bag," said Daisy.
"Me and *Tommy Toothless* here are having
a— Wait, did you say 'her'?"

Gap-tooth Jack
turned slowly towards
the dangling Skeleton
Keys. The glow of
moonlight from the
window illuminated
the boy's face.

"By my bones, it *is*,"
Skeleton Keys muttered
in dread. "It is Emily."

Excuse the intrusion, dallywanglers, but it is my dearest hope that you are enjoying *The Legend of Gap-tooth Jack*. Though I did not mean to mislead, this tall tale's title is not as straight-frontward as it might have seemed ... for it appears that Gap-tooth Jack is none other than Emily, the girl who imagined and unimagined none other than Ol' Mr Keys!

To explain: Emily did not choose the name – nor the life – of Gap-tooth Jack. Emily never knew her parents, but she suited life at neither the orphanage nor the workhouse. She lived as the forgotten did – in the shadows of the city's rookeries. But Emily had a skill – she was the most flabbergasting *thief* the city had ever seen. Why, she could steal a necklace from a neck as easily as a bone from a dog's mouth – and then disappear before anyone noticed! And, like the heroes of yester-yore,

Emily shared the spoils of thievery with those who, like her, were not born into the shine of favour. She was as bold as she was cunning, carving the shape of a key into the doors of those houses she had robbed, to prove there was no lock she could not defeat. Before long, Emily's exploits became legendary and, thanks to a less-than generous allocation of teeth, the mysterious thief became known throughout the city as 'Gap-tooth Jack'.

But Emily had a gift greater than her light fingers – her *imagination*. She imagined IFs not just to keep her company, but to *help* her ... the flying beetle, Chuckaboo, to guide her through the city, and, in time, a dapper 'n' daring skeleton whose key-tipped fingers could open *any* door ... even those to hidden worlds and secret places.

And, of course, Emily's IFs did not stay imaginary for long! Chuckaboo was unimagined first and, when the time was right, Emily imagined Ol' Mr Keys so wildly and so well that I suddenly became as real as eyebrows!

But alas, that is impossible … I *cannot* be unimagined. For although I am here talking to you now, I have, in the tale you have come to know as *The Legend of Gap-tooth Jack*, just encountered Emily by way of *the Key to Time*, thus breaking rules one to eleven of time travel – *Never Bump Into Your Own Past*.

The End of Everything is upon us! It seems all that remains is for the universe to explode into a billion, billion bits. Emily will never unimagine me and so I cannot be here, talking to you in this very moment.

Time travel really is the most confuddling mess.

And so, farewell, dallywanglers! It seems this story is well and truly over.

... Or is it?

Is what you imagine to be real, always real?
Do all stories begin and end as you expect?
Is everything you are told true? Or might
this tale take a turn even Ol' Mr Keys was not
expecting?

For, as I may have mentioned before,
strange things can happen when imaginations
run wild...

CHAPTER TWELVE

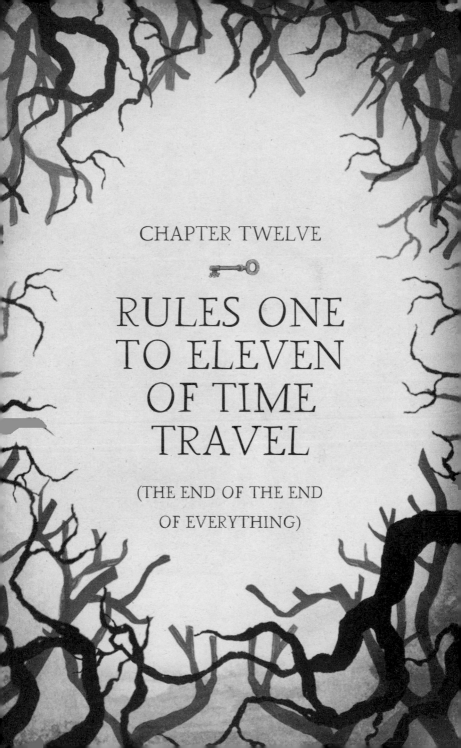

RULES ONE TO ELEVEN OF TIME TRAVEL

(THE END OF THE END OF EVERYTHING)

"I'm hard to catch, but if you do
You might just find that I've caught you!"
—*Gap-tooth Jack*

"Emily? As in, that Emily?" blurted Daisy as she glowered at the boy. "You're Emily?"

"How do you know my – that name?" gasped Gap-tooth Jack – or rather, Emily – as her beetle buzzed frantically around her head. "What in the name of my dear, departed teeth is goin' on?"

"Nothing! No one!" screeched Skeleton Keys in panic, quite certain that Everything was about to end. "Please, come no closer!"

"Silly, stupid bone-bag, you followed your

nose to the one person you said we couldn't bump into!" said Daisy. "Did 'Gap-tooth Jack' not ring any bells?"

"I have never even *heard* that name!" replied Skeleton Keys in a desperate whisper. "I only ever knew her as— I mean, nothing! Do not mind me! Please be on your way!"

"Hold your horseshoes, the pair of you," Emily said, pocketing Wordy Gerdy's pen as she edged towards the dangling skeleton. "I've never told my name to another living soul. Who *are* you?"

"Why, my name is – uh, Bones! Yes, that is it – Bartholomew Bones!" shrieked Skeleton Keys. "Now, please, not a step closer!"

Emily peered suspiciously at "Bartholomew Bones" – though the scarf was still wrapped around his head, there was something more than a little familiar about this intruder.

"Wait, I *know* you..." Emily muttered,

slowly reaching her hand towards the net.

"No, stay back – reality teeters on the brink of obliteration! And I have the most rottering cold!" howled the skeleton, squirming helplessly as Emily reached a hand into the net. Skeleton Keys screamed. "Stop, do not—"

But it was too late. Emily grabbed the scarf wrapped around Skeleton Key's head ... and pulled. It spun away in a coil, revealing his skull in all its bony glory.

"Can't be..." uttered Emily, aghast. "Mr Keys?"

"No, no! What have you done?" cried Skeleton Keys. "I have bumped into my own past! Run, run from the bumping! Run from the End of Everything!"

Everyone froze as Skeleton Keys writhed helplessly inside the net. He yanked and pulled, grunting and gasping. After a few more moments, his exertions began to slow, until finally he gave up with a feeble shrug.

There was a long pause.

Then silence.

Then an awkward moment.

Then another pause.

"I confess, I thought the End of Everything would be a bit more dramatic," Skeleton Keys said at last.

"Ugh, I *knew* it!" Daisy snapped. "Look around, you barmy bag of bones – 'everything' is fine."

"Can it be...?" Skeleton Keys murmured. "Reality has *not* sneezed itself to pieces?"

"Not even a bit – I'll bet my backwards head that *Nancy Neverwash* here made up that rule to stop you living in the past," said Daisy. She sighed as she glanced around the gloomy attic. "Which is literally what we're doing right now."

"Cheese 'n' biscuits, what grinnering luck! Everything has not ended!" cried Skeleton Keys. "Why, 'tis the End of the End of Everything!"

"Mr Keys? Is that really you?" said Emily. She kicked a makeshift lever in the floor to release the net that tethered Skeleton Keys, sending him crashing to the floor with a

THUMP.

"Would you look at that! Mr Keys, as real as a hot meal!" Emily uttered in awe, gazing down at Skeleton Keys as her beetle landed, clickety-clacking, on top of her head. "Yeah, *just* like you, Chuckaboo – from inside my head to right in front of my eyes!"

"Indeed, but with added time travel," said Skeleton Keys, untangling himself from the net and getting to his feet. He gazed wistfully into the face of the girl who imagined him – and unimagined him – all those years ago. "You are quite the sight for sore eye sockets, Emily. I did not think I would – *could* ever see you again."

"Again? I've only just laid eyes upon you this minute," Emily said.

"Ah, yes, since in the past, which is currently our present, I have not yet been unimagined," explained Skeleton Keys. "The me you see – that is to say, I – travelled from the future."

"*We* travelled from the future," Daisy corrected him. "And we didn't come here for a reunion tour – we came to get his keys back."

"Your keys?" Emily looked down at the skeleton's fingers.

"What happened to them?"

"Ghoul-girl happened," Daisy growled.

"That ghostie from the square?" said Emily, taking the pen out of her pocket. Her beetle let out a nervous chitter. "You said it, Chuckaboo – this is making my head spin."

"All you need to know is that Ol' Mr Keys is at your service and by your side, where I belong," said Skeleton Keys.

"We *don't* belong here," snapped Daisy. "What about ghoul-girl? What about being stuck in the smelliest bit of the past ever?"

"Emily and Ol' Mr Keys, back together for one more adventure!" Skeleton Keys declared with oblivious glee. "One hundred more! One thousand! One—"

"No," interrupted Daisy. "You promised. You promised you'd get us home."

"I am home! I mean, *we* are home – you can join us, of course, Daisy!" the skeleton said, although he did not take his eyes off Emily. "It will be just like the old days! Which will also be the new days."

"Sounds like a plan to me, Mr Keys," Emily grinned.

"It sounds like a *silly, stupid plan*," Daisy insisted. "How are you going to go on adventures without your keys?"

"My what? Oh, those," said the skeleton, glancing at his hands. With a shrug, he added, "Details! The point is that the adventure can begin again, for the first time! This is perfect – this is destiny! This is—"

"*Funnyface,*" said Emily.

"Exactly! Wait, what?" said Skeleton Keys. Emily stared past him, unblinking, to the window. Skeleton Keys turned and peered through the broken pane.

On the next rooftop across a wide, deep drop stood the grinning monster, Funnyface.

"Crumcrinkles!" cried Skeleton Keys. "We are discovered."

"There's not much hidden about our hideout any more, is there, Chuckaboo?" said Emily, her beetle jumping up and down on her head.

"Curse me for a saddle-goose!" said Skeleton Keys. "I fear that rough-handed rugslugger followed us here."

"Pfff, *I've* got stealth mode," tutted Daisy. "Maybe *Smellinda* here should have imagined someone less follow-able."

Funnyface stood as still as a statue, his impossible grin fixed to his face. Emily's beetle let out a clickety-clack so loud and fearful it echoed around the attic.

"Don't panic, Chuckaboo," said Emily. "That clown'll never get across the gap..."

Then, as if on cue, Funnyface bent his knees, arched his back ...

... and jumped.

143

CHAPTER THIRTEEN

FUNNYFACE ATTACKS

(THE UNIMAGINING OF SKELETON KEYS)

"My name is not Funnyface!"
—Hilario Flatulenté, clown

Time seemed to stand still as Emily watched Funnyface leap across the gap between the two buildings. For a split second, she was quite sure he could not reach them, but less than a moment later:

"Dogs 'n'—"

CRASH!

Funnyface smashed through the window. The monster landed in a shower of shattered glass and splintered window frame.

"Daisy!" cried Skeleton Keys. "Get Emily out of here!"

"Oh, so now *Sir Grinsalot* is back and spoiling for a fight, I'm useful?" Daisy replied. "Not this time, bone-bag. *You're* the one who wanted adventure. You sort it out."

With that, she turned invisible.

"Daisy!" cried Skeleton Keys as the monster loomed over him. Funnyface glared at him for a moment, his wide grin fixed to his face. Then he spun towards Emily and raised his clawed hands to strike.

"Crumcrinkles..." Emily muttered.

Skeleton Keys did not hesitate – he threw himself on to the monster's back and wrapped his arms around his neck. "Back, you foulsome funny-man!" he cried as Funnyface clawed at the skeleton, thrashing wildly and hitting himself repeatedly in the head.

As Chuckaboo scuttled under her cap, Emily set about doing what she always did when trouble struck – looking for an escape route. With Funnyface blocking the window, she raced for the door that Daisy had so worryingly locked.

"Blasted back-to-front girl, I would've *given* you the pen...!" Emily grumbled as Daisy sulked, invisibly, in a corner of the attic. She checked her pocket for her lock pick, but then she remembered it was still in her jacket, lying somewhere under the wreckage of the clock tower.

"Emily, flee!" cried the skeleton as he clung to the clown monster's neck. Suddenly, he felt Funnyface's huge hand clamp around his head. A moment later the monster flung him across the room like a rag doll. Emily ducked as he flew over her head and crashed into the door. As the skeleton slumped to the floor,

Funnyface spotted Wordy Gerdy's pen held tightly in Emily's hand. He rounded on her, hot breath puffing out from between his teeth.

"Looks like you got me bang to rights, Funnyface," Emily said, hiding the pen behind her back as she pressed herself against the door. "I take my hat off to you..."

With that, Emily whipped off her cap and held it out – Funnyface glanced down to see Emily's beetle fly out from inside. The startled monster stumbled back as Chuckaboo buzzed furiously around his face ... but he was not startled for long. In a flash, he brought a massive, hairy hand down upon the beetle, sending him spiralling dizzily to the floor.

"Chuck!" Emily cried.

Funnyface lifted his foot over Chuckaboo – and then brought it down with a ground-shaking thud.

"Chuckaboo!" Emily cried. "You monster!"

"See what happens when you take *pen*?" hissed a voice. A faint green glow appeared behind the looming Funnyface as Wordy Gerdy floated through the shattered attic window. "Gerdy's, not yours! Funnyface, take pen."

Funnyface's fixed grin did not waver as he stomped towards Emily. With tears in her eyes, Emily held Wordy Gerdy's pen over her head.

"You want this, you pair of monsters? Here!" she cried, and threw it as hard as she could into a shadowy corner of the attic. It clattered between two floorboards.

"Not again, pen! Funnyface, find!" shrieked Wordy Gerdy. Funnyface spun around like a dog watching a flying stick and stomped after the pen. Within moments he was tearing up floorboards with his claws.

With the ghost and the monster distracted, Emily turned back to the door. She grabbed the handle and pulled, hoping the old wood might give way, but the door wouldn't budge. For the first time in as long as she could remember, fear took hold. She looked down at the limp body of Skeleton Keys and wished more than anything that his fingers were as she'd always imagined them – each tipped with a remarkable key.

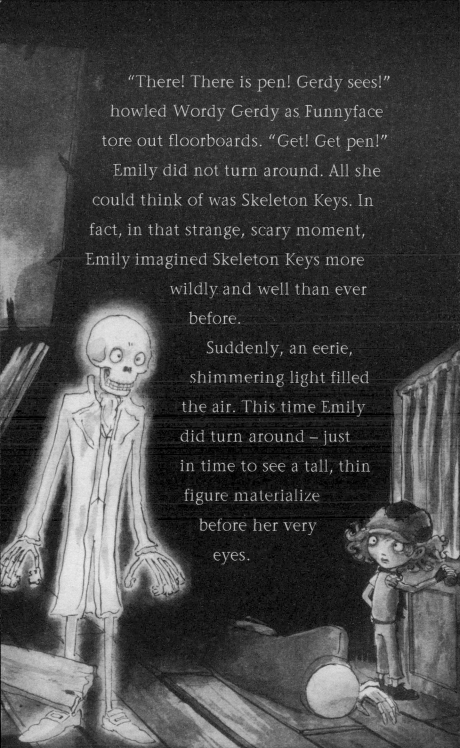

"There! There is pen! Gerdy sees!"
howled Wordy Gerdy as Funnyface
tore out floorboards. "Get! Get pen!"
Emily did not turn around. All she
could think of was Skeleton Keys. In
fact, in that strange, scary moment,
Emily imagined Skeleton Keys more
wildly and well than ever
before.

Suddenly, an eerie,
shimmering light filled
the air. This time Emily
did turn around – just
in time to see a tall, thin
figure materialize
before her very
eyes.

"Greetings!" said the figure, flashing his key-tipped fingers.

"Can't be..." Emily gasped.

But it was.

It was another Skeleton Keys.

"Mr – Mr Keys?" gasped Emily as the newly unimagined Skeleton Keys stood over her. Moonlight from the window silhouetted the skeleton's ten key-tipped fingers.

"Grinnering to see you, my dear ankle-sprout!" said the Other Skeleton Keys. He patted himself down with his key-tipped fingers. "Is it me, or does everything suddenly feel confuddlingly *solid*?" He turned back to examine his surroundings. "Where are we? I do not recall your imagination being so filled with murkish and miserable— MONSTER!"

At the sight of Funnyface, the Other Skeleton Keys let out a scream so filled with fear that it shook the foundations of the hideout. The skeleton watched in trembling horror as Funnyface dug Wordy Gerdy's pen out from between two floorboards. With a bow, he handed it to the ghoulish unimaginary.

"How Gerdy missed pen! How Gerdy missed *writing*," Wordy Gerdy cried, turning on Emily. "Funnyface, bring them to Gerdy..."

"Mr Keys, get us out of here!" Emily pleaded as Funnyface stomped towards them. "Your keys!"

"M-my what? Cheese 'n' biscuits, y-yes, of course!" said the Other Skeleton Keys, shaking with fear. He lifted his hand to the keyhole but his keys clattered uselessly around the edge of the lock.

"Hurry!" Emily cried. At last, the Other Skeleton Keys shoved his right thumb into the lock.

CLICK
CLUNK.

Emily swung open the door and together they dragged the unconscious Skeleton Keys through. Then, as the monster leaped towards them, the Other Skeleton Keys grabbed the door handle.

"Wait!" Emily cried. "What about Dais—"

But it was too late. The Other Skeleton Keys pulled the door shut.

CHAPTER FOURTEEN

SKELETON KEYS, MEET SKELETON KEYS

(ESCAPE TO IMAGINATION)

*"Don't know my place, don't know my station
All I know's imagination!"*
—Gap-tooth Jack

keleton Keys woke up to find his own skull staring back at him.

"Greetings," said the Other Skeleton Keys. "My name is Keys ... Skeleton Keys."

"What a coincidence, so is mine," replied Skeleton Keys as the other skeleton helped him to his feet. "However, your timely unimagining is not at all how I remember coming into the world. Cheese 'n' biscuits, have I altered the past and changed the future? Time travel is *so* confudd— Wait, where are we? Where is Emily?"

Skeleton Keys looked around. All he could see was darkness and fog. Then there she was – Emily, crouched in the darkness, hugging her knees as she quietly sobbed.

"Emily! Are you hurt?" he asked.

"Yeah … my heart's broke," Emily replied, tears threatening to clean her cheeks. "That clown squashed Chuckaboo."

"Crybaby," said Daisy, and the girl with the backwards head suddenly appeared.

"Daisy, there you are!" said Skeleton Keys.

"Oh, now you remember me," Daisy sighed. "Out of sight, out of mind…"

"I remember you *vanishing* in Emily's hour of need," Skeleton Keys chided her. "Dogs 'n' cats, Daisy, if you are not going to be helpful, then—"

"Then what? You'll run off with Nancy Neverwash? She's got her own bag of bones now – she doesn't need you any more." With that, Daisy pushed past both skeletons and held out her hand to Emily. "Yours, I believe."

Daisy opened her hand. There, dazed but intact, was Emily's beetle, Chuckaboo.

"Chuck! You're alive!" Emily cried, scooping Chuckaboo up in her hands. The beetle clicked weakly. "How? I saw Funnyface squash you like a bug..."

"I grabbed him before Funnyface stomped on him, obviously," Daisy replied. "You owe me for life, by the way. Now stop crying like a crybaby or I'll tread on him myself."

"Thank you!" cried Emily, wiping her eyes. She grabbed Daisy and gave her the first hug she'd ever had. "Thank you until the cows come home and my head falls off!"

"Ugh, get off me," Daisy groaned, squirming free. "All I care about is getting home to— Wait, where are we?"

"Seems awfully familiar..." said Emily, peering into the light-swallowing fog. Without thinking, she pursed her lips and blew – enough to snuff out a candle. The fog vanished in an instant, and the strange blackness parted like a wave. They found themselves on a small, grassy island, surrounded by a dark, crystalline ocean; the waves rose and fell as if they were breathing.

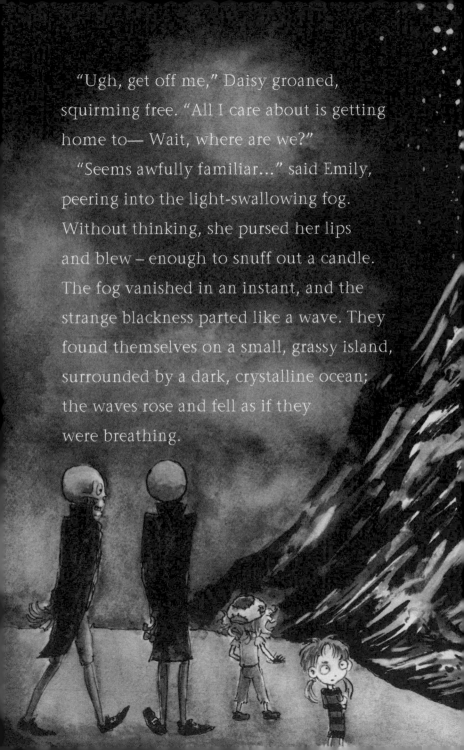

Then, as the sea touched the horizon, it
appeared to reach upwards to become a vast
mountain range, transforming again into a sky
and a galaxy of stars, which shimmered and
danced with light. It was as if there was no
beginning or end to any of it.

"Crumcrinkles, I would know this place
anywhere," said Skeleton Keys aghast. "It is
the most wonderfilling place imaginable.
It is my home."

"*Our* home," said the Other Skeleton Keys. "We are inside Emily's imagination."

"Inside my head?" exclaimed Emily, cradling Chuckaboo in her palm.

"That is where *the Key to Imagination* takes us, after all – to the world of your imaginings," the Other Skeleton Keys said, sticking up his thumb.

"Truth be told, that key will open a door to *any* imagination," Skeleton Keys corrected him. "But of all the imaginations I have encountered in my adventures, yours is still the most flabbergasting, Emily."

Emily grinned. "Well, then, let's have a proper look, shall we?"

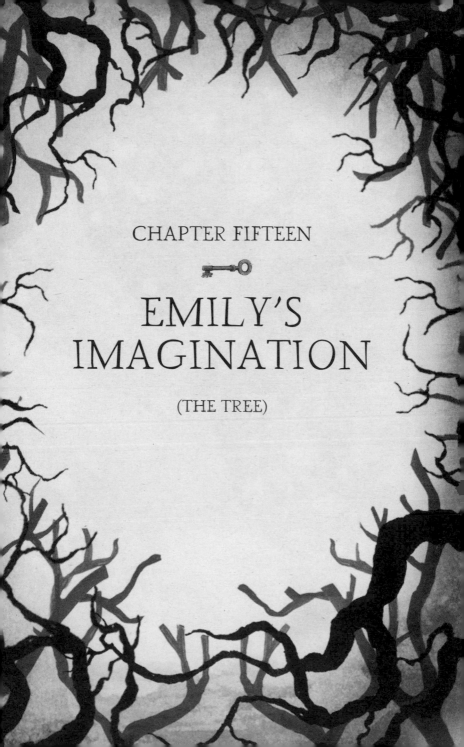

CHAPTER FIFTEEN

EMILY'S IMAGINATION

(THE TREE)

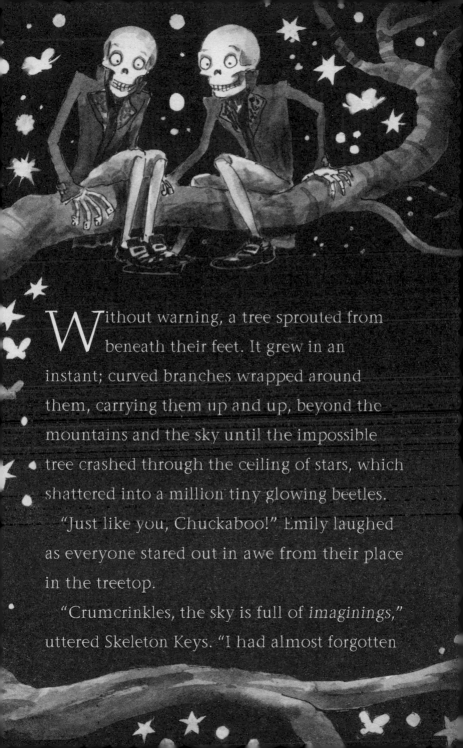

Without warning, a tree sprouted from beneath their feet. It grew in an instant; curved branches wrapped around them, carrying them up and up, beyond the mountains and the sky until the impossible tree crashed through the ceiling of stars, which shattered into a million tiny glowing beetles.

"Just like you, Chuckaboo!" Emily laughed as everyone stared out in awe from their place in the treetop.

"Crumcrinkles, the sky is full of *imaginings*," uttered Skeleton Keys. "I had almost forgotten how flabbergasting this all is."

Sure enough, there were figments of Emily's wild imagination as far as the eye could see. Immense, gleaming whales swam through the air surrounded by golden clouds comprising thousands of shimmering ethereal birds. A great airship seemed to pump like a beating heart as it made its way overhead, while herds of galloping horses emerged from nowhere, their hoof beats creating explosions of light and colour.

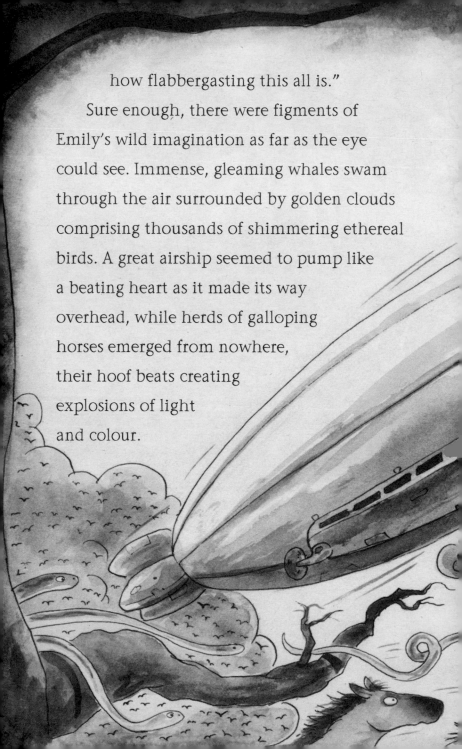

Stranger
creatures
appeared
too – silvery
snakes that
rippled like
water ... blue-striped
monsters whose roars
painted colours in the
air ... clanking, mechanical
men with steam pumping out

169

of their
numerous
arms and legs.
In the distance,
houses grew from
nothing and whirled around each
other to form towns and cities, and
far-off lands took form and vanished in
moments. Indeed, a hundred wild ideas
filled the void at any one time –

floating, flying, swimming and
soaring across a sky-scape of
endless possibilities.

"I don't see what all the fuss is about,"
tutted Daisy, shuffling sulkily on her branch.
"Let's get out of here."

"B-back to the real world?"
whimpered the Other Skeleton Keys.
"Cheese 'n' biscuits, need I remind
you about the *monster*?"

"I'm sorry to unimagine
you into all that
monstrous madness, Mr
Keys," said Emily. "It
was hardly fair, what
with you being such a
scaredy-bones 'n' all..."

"Indeed, I had almost
forgotten that you imagined me
as such a fretful fellow-me-chap,

171

Emily," noted Skeleton Keys. He glanced disdainfully at his past self. "It is hard to believe I was ever so wet behind the ear-canals."

"Better that than *past my prime*," scoffed the Other Skeleton Keys, showily plucking a leaf from a nearby branch.

"Past my prime? I have not aged a day in a dozen decades," insisted Skeleton Keys. "And at least I am no unseasoned *newbones* who is barely a minute unimagined."

"And at least *I* am not falling apart at the keys," sneered the Other Skeleton Keys. "I cannot help but notice that you do not have any."

"They were taken from me!" Skeleton Keys snapped, feeling thoroughly self-conscious about his keyless fingers. "I would be my old – I mean, my *whole* self, if not for that grim ghost rewriting me with her punishing pen. How else do you think we ended up in the past?"

"Well, fret not," said the Other Skeleton Keys pointedly. "With my fantabulant *Key to Time*, I can send you back to *when* you belong."

"Ugh, why didn't I think of that earlier?" Daisy piped up. "This new bone-bag can send us to our own time. We can leave them to sort out Wordy Gerdy and go home."

"Leave, without my keys? Out of the questioning," said Skeleton Keys.

"You didn't care about your keys two minutes ago," grunted Daisy. "All you cared about was hanging out with *her*."

"Well, we could all just stay here, in my imagination – I'd be literally out of my mind to leave!" Emily chuckled, effortlessly jumping from one tree branch to another. "My imaginings are my favourite things, but I never actually thought I could step foot inside them. Also, cake! Let's have some cake!"

With that, two pigeons riding a tandem
bicycle appeared out of thin air to deliver a

freshly imagined
fruitcake,
which flew
obediently
into Emily's
mouth.

"Delicious!"
she laughed,
wiping cake
crumbs (and a good deal of grime) from her
face. "Still hungry, though..."

"I am afraid anything you consume will fill
your mind, but not your belly," said Skeleton
Keys. "All these things *seem* real, but if you
began your existence in the real world, you
cannot survive here."

"I can't?" Emily said. She smacked her lips
together, the taste of cake disappearing like

a dream. She gave her beetle another stroke, and it clickety-clacked contentedly. "And while we're here, I suppose Wordy Gerdy is still making trouble back home?"

"Dogs 'n' cats, I am sure she is causing the most horrible huff 'n' hubbub," replied Skeleton Keys. "With her pen back in her possession, she will set about rewriting the whole city ... unless somebody stops her."

Emily sat down on a tree branch and looked around, taking in the endless world of her own imagination. She took a long breath.

"Then I guess that somebody had better be us," she said at last. "It's time to go home."

CHAPTER SIXTEEN

CITY OF
MONSTERS

(RUNNING OUT OF IDEAS)

"Monsters lurking in my head
Might cause me some alarm
But they're not real, what e'er I feel
They cannot do me harm!"
—Gap-tooth Jack

"I will return us to the real world on one condition," the Other Skeleton Keys exclaimed, pacing nervously up and down the branches of Emily's imagination tree. "That I lay not a single eye socket on that rumbleshoving monster."

"Bones 'n' buckles, was I ever so shiver-livered?" said Skeleton Keys. "I may not have keys, but at least I have a spine."

"I have a spine!" insisted the Other Skeleton Keys. "It pokes out of my coat when I bend over."

"Ugh, two bone-bags is one too many, at least," groaned Daisy.

"They're a handful, all right," replied Emily, her beetle clickety-clacking from the top of her head. Then she took a deep, serious breath. "Right, let's get started..."

With a single thought, the titanic tree vanished, depositing them back on the island below. Emily imagined a wooden door, which immediately appeared in front of her.

"Everybody ready?" she asked. "This might turn into quite the adventure."

Her beetle came to rest upon her index finger. He lowered his head and let out a single soft click. "Don't be daft, Chuck – of course I understand."

"Understand what?" said Daisy.

"My friend Chuckaboo says he's reminded of the rare comfort that comes from existing as a figment of my imagination. He asks if he can stay here, for now at least," Emily explained.

"I do not see why not," said Skeleton Keys, shooting a sideways glance at his past self. "*Any* unimaginary may return to the realm of imaginings, should they feel unready for the real world. All they need is *the Key to Imagination*."

"Well, I'm going to miss you, little beetle. But as long as you're in my imagination, we'll never be apart," Emily said with a smile. She held her beetle up to her lips and kissed him gently.

"Eww," said Daisy.

"Good luck, Chuck," added Emily, and held out her finger. Her beetle paused for a moment, before letting out a last clickety-clack and taking to the air. Emily watched him disappear into the sky and blinked away a tear.

"All right, Mr Keys, let's get back to reality."

"Sticks 'n' stones, do not say I did not warn you," sighed the Other Skeleton Keys, and slipped *the Key to Imagination* in the lock. There was a

CLICK
CLUNK

and Emily pushed the door open.

"We may have been worrying over nothing," she whispered, stepping back into her now-abandoned attic. "It doesn't look like anything's changed..."

"This is the bit where you look out of the window, dummy," said Daisy as the two Skeleton Keys followed her into the room. Emily crept over to the window and peered out.

"Oh *my*," she said. "I think Wordy Gerdy might be running out of ideas..."

Below them, the streets teemed ...

... with monsters.

A horrifying horde of impossible, beastly creatures filled the rookeries. Emily watched one misshapen monster after another lumber down the street, each distorted and inhuman in their own unique way.

"I take back everything I said about ghoul-girl," said Daisy. "This is *great*."

"Daisy, stop enjoying the villainy," said Skeleton Keys, peering down at the monstrous mob. "Crumcrinkles, Wordy Gerdy has already rewritten dozens."

"This is *literally* my worst nightmare," the Other Skeleton Keys said, his bones rattling with fear. "What now? We cannot take on a city chock-brimming with monsters!"

"We don't need to – all we need is that pen," said Emily. "Now I don't want to brag, but I'm a half-decent thief, so stealing I can do. But Wordy Gerdy has an army on her side now. If I'm to take the pen, I'll need you to create a distraction – something big."

Skeleton Keys looked at the Other Skeleton Keys.

"Leave that to me," he said, thoughtfully tapping his fingers against his chin. "He may have the keys ... but I have a plan."

CHAPTER SEVENTEEN

THE PLAN

(POSSIBLY)

> *"I laugh in the face of danger*
> *I snort in the nose of threat*
> *I chuckle in the ears of peril*
> *And seldom break a sweat!"*
> —*Gap-tooth Jack*

Halfway across the city in the town square, Wordy Gerdy floated above the wreckage of the fallen clock tower. At her command, her monstrous army gathered round to protect her and her precious pen. She whirled the pen through the air, scrawling the same word again and again.

MONSTER
MONSTER
MONSTER

Her creations rapidly filled the square. They had begun to crawl and clamber over each other for room. Even Wordy Gerdy's first monster, Funnyface, climbed on to the toppled clock tower to escape the monstrous multitude.

"Monster! Monster!" Wordy Gerdy repeated. She had made so many, she was starting to forget how to write anything else. She spun in the air as she searched for someone else to transform.

Then, suddenly, they appeared.

From the door of a small sweet shop at the far end of the square emerged not one but two Skeleton Keys.

"You!" Wordy Gerdy hissed. "And you!"

"Greetings! To the rewritten, the unchanged and everything in between!" declared Skeleton Keys as he and his trembling counterpart stood either side of the door. "And greetings to you, Wordy Gerdy! I see you have been busy, but you seem to be repeating yourself.

Could you be suffering from rewriter's block?"

"Monsters! Get them!" she cried, pointing at the skeletons with her pen. A hundred monsters rounded on the two skeletons and, led by the grinning Funnyface, began lumbering towards them.

"I-I know you said you had a plan, Mr Keys," whimpered the Other Skeleton Keys, "but surely this cannot be it!"

"Plan?" Skeleton Keys pointed at the keyhole. "Who needs a plan when you have the *Key to Possibility?*"

"P-possibility?" stuttered the Other Skeleton Keys as the rumble of monsters got closer. "Which one is that again?"

"On your right hand, count two fingers from your thumb," said Skeleton Keys. "Fret not, Mr Keys – anything is possible when *the Key to Possibility* makes anything possible! Possibly."

"That m-makes me feel much better," the Other Skeleton Keys replied, his trembling finger hovering by the lock.

"Steady, Mr Keys – not yet," said Skeleton Keys. "Wait until they are closer…"

The Other Skeleton Keys' bones rattled uncontrollably as the monstrous horde closed in. They would be on them in seconds.

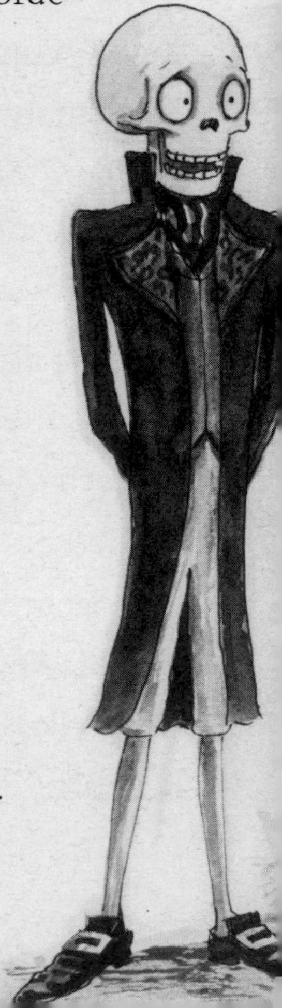

"N-now?" he asked.

"Not yet."

"Now?"

"Not yet."

"Now?"

"Not ye— Wait, yes, now. NOW!"

The Other Skeleton Keys jammed the key into the lock. He twisted it with a CLICK CLUNK and turned the handle.

The pressure behind the door pushed it open
so fast that the Other Skeleton Keys was
knocked off his feet.

Then from inside the door came a tidal
wave.

A tidal wave ...
... of pens.

CHAPTER EIGHTEEN

PENS!

(EMILY SWINGS IN)

Gap-tooth Jack! Gap-tooth Jack!
You took my stuff, now give it back!

The pens poured out in their thousands ...
millions ... *billions* ... a torrent of pens
of all shapes, sizes and colours, surging out of
the door with such force and in such vast
numbers that they swept even the
largest monsters off their feet
and carried

them across the square. Within moments, Funnyface and the monstrous horde were engulfed in the wave and swallowed up.

"Pens..." noted the Other Skeleton Keys in relief as he got to his feet. "How ironic."

"Possibly!" replied Skeleton Keys with a dry chuckle.

Wordy Gerdy, meanwhile, had managed to float clear of the cascade, her precious pen pressed to her chest.

"Funnyface! Monsters!" she shrieked as her monsters vanished beneath the wave.

"That's something you don't see every day," said Emily from her rooftop perch, high above the square. As she looped one end of a long rope, Daisy clung to her back, her arms around Emily's neck. "All set, Daisy?"

"My head is backwards," groaned Daisy. "And I can *still* smell you."

"I'll take that as a yes," Emily grinned.

Daisy held on tighter as she turned invisible. Then Emily whirled the looped end of the rope above her head and flung it into the air. It caught upon the neck of a gargoyle on the other side of the square. "Hang on," she said. Then she bent her knees, arched her back ... and jumped.

Wordy Gerdy did not even see Emily coming – she was too busy worrying about her monsters drowning in pens. But then she heard Emily's cry.

"Evening, ghostie! And thank you for your kind donation!"

The ghost writer spun in the air just in time for Emily to swing past her. The gap-toothed girl reached out for the pen ... and then missed it by an inch.

"*Stinker!*" Wordy Gerdy yelled as Emily leaped from the rope and landed on the edge of the pen cascade by the two Skeleton Keys. "You missed Gerdy!" she cried victoriously.

"Missed, missed! Missed!"

"Are you sure about that?" Emily replied.

Gerdy looked down at her hand.

Her pen was gone.

"No, oh no!" she cried, casting her eyes down to the ocean of pens. Then she rounded on Emily. "Stinker, give! Give pen!"

Emily shrugged and held out her empty hands.

"Who, me? I don't have it," she said. "Maybe you dropped it?"

"Dropped...?" Wordy Gerdy whimpered

as she gazed down at the mountain of pens. "No, no, NO!"

Wordy Gerdy's shriek echoed around the square and back at her. She dived into the mass of pens, swimming against the tide of monsters that were trying to dig themselves free. After a few moments she burst out of the depths and then immediately dived in again. Up and down she went, each time crying out in increasing desperation...

"PEN!"

Finally, Wordy Gerdy burst out of the mass of pens and hovered in the air.

"Too many ... too many!" she howled in miserable horror.

"Wordy Gerdy, your rottering reign of rewriting is over!" cried Skeleton Keys, pushing the door to the sweet shop shut and finally ending the torrent of pens. "Undo your doings, or by my bones, you will never see your pen again."

"Bad Mr Bones! Nasty trick!" Wordy Gerdy whined, scooping pens up in her hands. "Please help ... where is pen?"

"We don't have it," said Emily. "She does."

"Surprise," said a voice. In an instant, Daisy reappeared in front of Skeleton Keys, Wordy Gerdy's pen in hand. "I know how to do stealing now. You didn't even notice me grab the pen out of your hand when Smellinda

swung past, did you?"

"Bad girl, give pen!" Gerdy snarled. She saw
Funnyface begin to claw his way out of the
mass of pens. "Look, Gerdy still has monsters!
Give pen, or—"

"Shut up," Daisy said.
"Undo it all, now. Do it, or I
will break your silly pen into
bits."

"Bad girl wouldn't!" Wordy Gerdy wailed, floating slowly towards Daisy. "Break pen and Mr Bones *never* gets his keys back. Bad girl wouldn't ... bad girl *couldn't*."

Daisy looked back at Skeleton Keys, on the edge of the ocean of pens, standing protectively in front of the girl who unimagined him. She stared at them for a long moment, and turned back to Wordy Gerdy.

"He won't mind – he's got everything he needs here, anyway," she said with a sigh. Then her face hardened. She grabbed the pen in both hands...

"STOP! Stop! Gerdy believes!" Gerdy cried. With that, she stuck her fingers in her ears and puffed out her cheeks. A second later came a

POP

– and everything changed.

CHAPTER NINETEEN

BACK TO
ABNORMAL

(EMILY'S OFFER)

'Tis the most confuddling thing!
By gift of wild imagining
I am sudden made as real as toes
Then forced to face most monstrous foes!
Adventures lie ahead, it seems
For Emily and Mr Keys!

Reality reset itself in an instant.

The echoing POP rang out over the city as Wordy Gerdy's work was undone. The first thing Emily and the two Skeleton Keys noticed was that the creatures crawling out of the mountain of pens were once again human. Even Funnyface had gone from monster to man in an instant. He immediately spotted the maddening sight of his nemesis: Gap-tooth Jack.

"*You again!*" he growled, clenching his fists. The second thing he saw, however, was a pair of living skeletons and a girl with a backwards head. Emily watched him slink in horror back into the shadows.

"Everything is back to abnormal ... or is it?" said Skeleton Keys, glancing tensely down at his fingers. He saw the air around his hands shimmer with an eerie light and then, one by one, his remarkable keys returned to the tips of his fingers. "By my buckles, I am restored to my former fantabulance! I am myself again!"

"I knew you were the real thing, Mr Keys," laughed Emily in delight.

"There, Gerdy has undone! Everything is back!" Gerdy cried. "Now, please, give pen..."

"Silly ghoul," Daisy noted, with a grimace. "I was *always* going to break it."

"Don't be daft, Daisy," said Emily, effortlessly swiping the pen from Daisy's hand. "Gerdy's writing may be wrong, but two wrongs don't make a right. This pen is part of who she is. It belongs to her."

"*What?*" howled Daisy.

"Horse 'n' cart, Emily, wait!" cried Skeleton Keys. "If you return her pen, Wordy Gerdy will begin her rottering revisions all over again."

"Is that true, Gerdy?" asked Emily, holding out the pen to the ghost writer. "If I give you back your pen, will you keep rewriting?"

"No! No, I—" began Wordy Gerdy, her trembling hand grasping for the pen. Then she paused and looked Emily straight in the eye. "Yes," she said. "If you give pen, Gerdy will write."

"See? She admitted it," Daisy huffed. "Break the silly pen, preferably over her head."

"Is not Gerdy's fault," Gerdy said, a glowing green tear running down her cheek. "Gerdy writes! It is what Gerdy does ... it is what Gerdy *is*."

"I understand – you didn't ask to be imagined

– or unimagined. But we just can't have you rewriting the whole world," Emily explained. She took off her cap and scratched her head, sending a cloud of dust into the air. At last, she asked, "Wordy Gerdy, what if you could go to a place where you could do all the rewriting you liked, and no one would bat an eyelid?"

"Where?" asked Wordy Gerdy.

Emily tapped the side of her head.

"Here," she said. "In my imagination."

"WHAT?" cried the two Skeleton Keys together.

"It's simple," Emily explained. "I give Wordy Gerdy back her pen and then we use *the Key to Imagination* to put her in my head. She can do all the writing she likes in there – I reckon my imaginings can take it."

"You would do that for Gerdy?" said Wordy Gerdy. "Why?"

"'Cause I know what it's like to have a wild

imagination," replied Emily. Then she slowly placed the pen in Wordy Gerdy's hand.

"Ugh, I'm not doing this all over again," Daisy groaned.

"Everything's going to be OK, Gerdy," said Emily softly. "Mr Keys, your key, if you please."

Both skeletons held out their key-tipped fingers.

"Ah, of course," said Skeleton Keys. "After you, Mr Keys."

The Other Skeleton Keys shook his head.

"No, after *you*," he said, looking down at his keys. "I-I find it rather confuddling trying to keep up with which key does what..."

Skeleton Keys shrugged and nodded all at once. "Practice makes perfect, Mr Keys. No one said being an unimaginary friend is easy ... but it is quite the adventure."

"I will take your word for it," muttered the

Other Skeleton Keys.

Skeleton Keys put his newly restored *Key to Imagination* into the lock on the sweet-shop door. He turned the key with a CLICK CLUNK and opened the door to reveal a wondrous world of wild imaginings.

"Ugh, not this dump again," grunted Daisy.

Emily turned to Wordy Gerdy.

"Welcome to my imagination, Gerdy," she said with a grin. "Make yourself at home."

CHAPTER TWENTY

UNREADY

(DECISIONS)

From The Important Thoughts of Mr S. Keys
Volume 10: The Key to Oblivion

The saddest thing is not to be gone,
it is to be forgot.

Not quite five minutes later, the two Skeleton Keys and Daisy stood outside the locked sweet-shop door, staring at Emily. Her eyes were closed and her mouth pursed in concentration. Dawn had yet to break across the city, and the air was cold and sharp.

"Ugh, can we go home now?" Daisy said at last.

"Patience, Daisy – Emily is having to contend with a new addition to her imagination," said Skeleton Keys. "We must think of her, for once."

"Right ... for once," sighed Daisy, folding her arms.

"So?" asked the Other Skeleton Keys. "How is Wordy Gerdy getting on in there?"

After a moment, Emily opened her eyes, and a wide, gap-toothed grin appeared on her face. "She's taking to it like a duck to water," she chuckled. "She's rewriting the place like crazy, but to be honest, it just makes things more interesting..."

"A grinnering relief," exclaimed the Other Skeleton Keys. "This horrible, horrible day is finally looking up."

"And what a day it's been!" laughed Emily. "I can't wait for our next adventure, Mr Keys."

"Nor I!" said Skeleton Keys. Then he glanced over at his past self. "Ah, but of course, she meant you."

"About that," the Other Skeleton Keys said. "I do not mean to throw a scupper in the works, Emily, but I may have to hold your horseshoes regarding ... adventures."

"What do you mean?" Emily said with a dusty scratch of her head.

"I am sorry," he replied. "But I fear I am *unready* to be unimaginary."

"Unready?" Emily repeated. "Of course you're ready – aren't you?"

"I just never expected the real world to be so very ... *real*. And also filled with monsters," explained the Other Skeleton Keys. He gestured to his future self. "*This* Mr Keys is bold and fearless and all the things I am not – all the things I do not think I can ever be. This is the unimaginary friend you need, Emily."

"I do not understand," said Skeleton Keys.

"I, too, wish to return to Emily's imagination," the Other Skeleton Keys said at last. "And I wish for you to take my place by

Emily's side – to be the me that I cannot."

Skeleton Keys could not contain his gasp.

"Me, be you?"

"Who better to take my place on a thousand wild, wonderfilled and unbearably spine-chillering adventures than an older, wiser, braver me?" said the Other Skeleton Keys.

"Mr Keys, are you sure?" asked Emily.

"I am as certain as sausages," the Other Skeleton Keys confirmed. "I want to go back."

"Well, I guess you didn't ask to be unimagined either, Mr Keys," said Emily a little sadly, and turned to Skeleton Keys. "What do you say, Mr Keys?"

"I ... I say it would be the most fantabulant honour of this or any existence," Skeleton Keys answered. Then he heard a huffing grunt and realized Daisy was standing right next to him. "Daisy, there you are! Where did you disappear off to?"

"I wasn't invisible," Daisy said. "You just didn't see me."

"Then you must have heard the fantabulant news," said Skeleton Keys. "I believe the three of us are destined for the most flabbergasting adventures."

"And I believe I'll miss you as much as my last fart," Daisy replied.

"Miss me?" said the skeleton. "What do you mean?"

"You want to live in the past? Go ahead – but not me," Daisy said. "I might as well be invisible when you're with Emily. Well, I decide when I'm invisible, not you."

"Daisy, it is not like that," insisted Skeleton Keys. "If Mr Keys does not wish to join Emily on her adventures, then I must. I have no choice."

Daisy walked over to the sweet-shop door.

"You always have a choice, dummy," she said. "Just send me home."

"Stay, Daisy, do!" Skeleton Keys added. "Crumcrinkles, there really is no need to—"

"Send. Me. Home," Daisy hissed, giving the skeleton an icy glare. "Do it, or I'll make you both wish you'd never met me."

Skeleton Keys knew better than to argue with the third most troublesome unimaginary he had ever met. Reluctantly he put *the Key to Time* into the door and turned.

CLICK

CLUNK.

Daisy shoved past him and opened the door. As Emily and the Other Skeleton Keys looked on, Daisy paused in the doorway.

"I – I will see you very soon," Skeleton Keys said. "For you, no time will have passed, but I will have lived a lifetime ... all over again."

"Our time's up, bone-bag. Just leave me alone," Daisy replied. "And have fun living in the past – you've been doing it long enough."

And with that, she pushed the door shut.

CHAPTER TWENTY-ONE

ABOUT TIME

(LEAVING THE PAST IN THE PAST)

A time long past but not forgot
A ghoulish foe, a fiendish plot
Pens and friends! Both new and old
And wild imaginings untold!
What's past is done, 'tis memory!
'Tis Gap-tooth Jack – and Emily!

Daisy found herself in the middle of the city ... the present-day metropolis of neon and noise that they had left behind on their way to the past. The thunderstorm was over – the last of the rain fell in a fine mist, and the morning sunshine was moments away.

She took a long breath of damp air and sighed. For the first time since she was unimagined, Daisy had no idea what to do next. She glanced back and saw that the door from which she'd emerged was now the entrance to a shop selling old clocks. The shop window was filled with timepieces of all shapes and sizes, which ticked and tocked at her through the glass. Daisy stood there for a long moment, watching time pass.

"Silly clocks," she said. "Stupid *time*."

She suddenly felt the need to break every single clock in the shop, and turned invisible in preparation for some mindless destruction. But then, as she reached for the door handle, there came a

CLICK
CLUNK.

The door suddenly swung open and a figure strode out – straight into Daisy.

"Dogs 'n' cats!" came a cry as Skeleton Keys stumbled backwards. "Daisy, is that you?"

"I thought I told you to leave me alone," Daisy replied, reappearing.

"You did indeed," said Skeleton Keys. "But

you also reminded me that everyone has a choice ... so I chose not to."

"You're *so* annoying," Daisy groaned. "So, how was the last two hundred years?"

"Truth be told, only seven minutes have passed for me since I last saw you," Skeleton Keys explained.

"What did you do with seven whole minutes?"

"As a matter of factly, I came to my senses. The moment you walked through that door, Daisy, I realized you were right."

"Obviously," she snorted. She scuffed the pavement with her foot and added, "Right about what?"

"About the first rule of time travel," replied the skeleton. "I am quite certain that Emily *did* invent that rule to dissuade me from going back to find her. If she had not, she knew I would have clung to the past, even as the future was there for the taking. We always have a choice – and I choose to leave the past in the past."

Daisy snorted. "What about Nancy Neverwash? Did you leave her all alone?"

"It took six and a half minutes, but I managed to convince the other Mr Keys not to return to Emily's imagination," explained the skeleton. "I told him that the wild and wonderfilling years I spent with Emily were the *making* of Ol' Mr Keys. I told him to be brave and embrace the adventure, and he might just turn out like me. And it must have worked, for here I am, as fantabulant as always!"

"Ugh, I *hate* time travel," Daisy groaned. "Anyway, what's this got to do with me?"

Skeleton Keys looked up into the sky. Dawn was breaking.

"Life is an adventure, Daisy. It is an as-yet

untold tale, with a beginning, a middle and an end. And if you will do me, a foolsome, unworthy and undeserving bag o' bones, the very great honour of remaining my friend—"

"Partner," Daisy corrected him.

"—Partner," repeated the skeleton, "then I am quite sure the best years of my life are not behind me – they are ahead. What do you say?"

Daisy looked up. The sun at last rose clear of the buildings and cast an orange glow over the city.

"I say it's about time," she said. "But no more living in the past."

"Quite so! After all, there is no time like the present," said Skeleton Keys. He closed the door to the clock shop and then raised his ten key-tipped fingers. "Where would you like to go?"

S o there we have it, dallywanglers! The truly unbelievable, unbelievably true tale of *The Legend of Gap-tooth Jack*. Didn't I tell you it was a hum-dum-dinger? It is an adventure I will never forget – though, thanks to the confuddlement of time travel, it did not turn out quite as I remember...

And speaking of forgetting – cheese 'n' biscuits! – it almost slipped my skull to mention young Kasper, with whom this story began. Rest assured that Daisy and I returned to Kasper's home to inform him of Wordy Gerdy's fate – and to let him know that she would not be returning. Bones 'n' buckles, the family breathed a sigh of relief, knowing that she was gone! Kasper, however, was more relieved that his unimaginary friend had found a new home in Emily's wild imagination. The real world was free of her, but Wordy Gerdy was finally free to be herself.

Meanwhile, our adventures in the past are done and dusty – now Daisy and I look to new adventures. What flabbergasting exploits does the future hold? I cannot imagine!

For it has been said, and it cannot be denied, that strange things can happen when imaginations run wild...

Until next time, until next tale, farewell!

Your servant in storytelling,

—SK

WANT TO FIND OUT ABOUT
SKELETON KEYS' NEXT ADVENTURE?

READ ON...

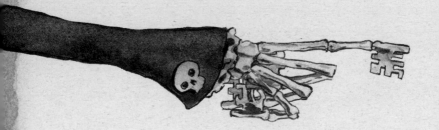

reetings! To gadarounds, chanternuts and rooklers! To the imaginary and the unimaginary! To the living, the dead and everyone in between, my name is Keys ... Skeleton Keys.

Hundreds of moons ago, I was an IF – an imaginary friend. Then, before I could say "Crumcrinkles", I was suddenly as real as feet! I had become unimaginary.

Now Ol' Mr Keys looks out for other IFs who find themselves suddenly unimagined, wherever they materialize! For these fantabulant fingers open doors to anywhere and elsewhere ... hidden worlds ... secret places ... doors to the limitless realm of all imagination.

These keys have opened a thousand doors and each door has led to an adventure! Dogs 'n' cats, the stories I could tell you...

But of course, it is a story you are waiting for! Well, fret not, dallywanglers – today's tall tale is such a hum-dum-dinger that it will make you question everything you believe – a tale so truly unbelievable that it must, unbelievably, be true.

This is Finnegan Twist. It is safe to say, which I do, that Finnegan lives in a world of his own. Even he is not sure why he so often escapes into his own imagination. But, wherever possible, Finnegan lets his mind wander to the wonderfilled world of his wild imaginings, in which he is the hero of his own story. It is a tale of a brave and valiant champion ... a tale of noble quests and dangers untold ... a tale of soaring into battle upon the back of a mighty, winged steed.

But, little does Finnegan know, his real life is about to become more adventuresome than he ever could have imagined.

For strange things can happen when imaginations run wild...

Our story begins in the quiet, oh-so slumberly village of Matching Trousers. It is autumn, and ruddy-reddish leaves strew quiet, tree-lined streets. Finnegan and his infant sister, Nellie, have recently moved to live with their grandmother. It is the end of their first week in the village, and life, though generally uneventful, is not without surprises...

Guy Bass is an award-winning author and semi-professional geek. He has written over thirty books, including the best-selling *Stitch Head* series (which has been translated into sixteen languages) *Dinkin Dings and the Frightening Things* (winner of a 2010 Blue Peter Book Award) *Spynosaur, Laura Norder: Sheriff of Butts Canyon, Noah Scape Can't Stop Repeating Himself, Atomic!* and *The Legend of Frog.*

Guy has previously written plays for both adults and children. He lives in London with his wife and imaginary dog. Find out more at guybass.com

Pete Williamson is a self-taught artist and illustrator.
He is best known for the much-loved *Stitch Head* series by
Guy Bass, and the award-winning *The Raven Mysteries*
by Marcus Sedgwick.

Pete has illustrated over sixty-five books by authors including
Francesca Simon, Matt Haig and Charles Dickens. Before that
he worked as a designer in an animation company (while
daydreaming about being a children's book illustrator).

Pete now lives in rural Kent with a big piano, a writer wife and
a dancing daughter. Find out more at petewilliamson.co.uk

Have you read *Stitch Head*?

'It's dark, monstrous fun!' Wondrous Reads

In Castle Grotteskew something BIG
is about to happen to someone SMALL.
Join a mad professor's first creation as
he steps out of the shadows into the
adventure of an almost lifetime...

Read all Stitch Head's adventures:

The Pirate's Eye

The Ghost of Grotteskew

THE SPIDER'S LAIR

The Beast of Grubbers Nubbin

THE MONSTER HUNTER

BRINGING THE CHARACTERS TO LIFE

Guy and Pete explain how the characters evolved...

Gaptooth Jack/Emily

GB: Pete did a few sketches of Emily and they all captured her spirit – bold, playful and cool-headed. It was just a matter of tweaking the design (I was particularly obsessed about the size of the gap between Emily's teeth) and getting rid of the eyepatch that I forgot I'd given her!

PW: Emily's a proper street urchin – resourceful and full of life, she's more than capable of making her way in the big city. The unruly hair, patterned and patched clothing and general healthy grubbiness captures her infectious energy. I wouldn't stand down wind of her though.

Wordy Gerdy

GB: Gerdy went through a ghostly transformation as
her design progressed – I love her floating hair and
blank, staring eyes. We ended up reducing the size of her
paranormal pen as it gets hidden or pocketed a lot in
the story.

PW: I first sketched a slightly grumpy, less eerie
character, but then remembered I'd drawn a dreamlike,
floating girl some years ago and was inspired to use her as
a model – though with even more hair. Her eyes became
wonderfully empty and strange, yet still expressive.

READ ABOUT SKELETON KEYS' OTHER ADVENTURES...

When Ben's imaginary friend, the Gorblimey, suddenly becomes real, Skeleton Keys is convinced the little monster is dangerous. But someone far more monstrous is out there, waiting to take revenge on Ben...

When Luna's family members start disappearing before her very eyes she thinks her ghostly granddad is to blame. But Skeleton Keys isn't so sure – he's certain something even more mysterious lurks in the shadows – something UNIMAGINARY.